WAR COLLEGE

...IT'S COMPLICATED.

BY

MARK DONAHUE

D!
DONAHUE
LITERARY PROPERTIES

Editing, Formatting, and Cover Design by Ebook Launch

Illustration by Marsha Donahue

First eBook and Paperback editions published in the United States of America by

Donahue Literary Properties, LLC, 2024.

www.DonahueLiteraryProperties.com

www.MarkRDonahue.com

Other Books by Mark Donahue

Last at Bat

Fat Girl

Golden Reich

Stats

Answer Man

PROLOGUE

The best way to describe the Vietnam War to a younger generation is to say, "It's complicated."

It was complicated back then too, in addition to being frustrating, disheartening, confusing, rage inducing, and, in far too many cases, fatal for 58,220 American soldiers who died in that war. An additional 300,000 were hospitalized with injuries, and hundreds of thousands more are still suffering from what we now call PTSD.

The book you are holding is described as historical fiction in that it blends accurate historical facts with stuff I made up or embellished about a single year in my life between June of 1965 and June of 1966. My story is not intended to deal with that time period in a strict biographical or historical sense, but rather focuses on a sliver of time when the war overshadowed the lives of millions of young men and women and their families. More importantly, it forced an entire generation to realize our government had lied to us. This realization is still impacting American citizens to this day.

Our government and many of its leaders continue to lie to us almost every day. Maybe they lied to us before the Vietnam War, but it was during the 1960s and 1970s we finally caught them red-handed.

Some of the characters you will meet are not real people but rather an amalgam of the hundreds of people I met during my year at Hiram Scott College, a "for-profit" school in Scottsbluff, Nebraska, back in the 1960s.

Some of the events depicted in the book actually occurred; some not so much. But even the embellished ones are based on facts, as I remember them to be.

Historical fiction is both an oxymoron and literary genre. It also possesses the unique potential to offend the sensibilities of both those who demand precise historical accuracy in their reading material, while also disappointing fiction lovers looking for a solely creative storyline filled only with figments of an author's vivid imagination. Yet, authors have relied on this genre for literally hundreds of years to tell fictional stories based on historical facts.

In the case of *War College*, I fell back on the axiom that one should write about what one knows. That's why, in part, I have written about baseball in *Last at Bat*; friendship in *Golden Reich*; and based on my three years working on The Hill in Washington, DC, the political shenanigans I witnessed firsthand in *Stats*. *Fat Girl* was based on a neighbor who suffered from obesity, and *Answer Man* came from my love of *The Twilight Zone* and Rod Serling. *War College*, however, is as close to my heart and my life as any I have written.

While this is not an autobiography, there are important parallels between this book and my own life. I attended Hiram Scott College on a basketball scholarship back in the '60s. Yes, the college was real and one of hundreds of "war colleges" that sprang up across the country during that time period—Google it.

Not all the students who attended these colleges did so to avoid the draft, but many, many did, *if* they could afford college. If they could *not* afford it, and they were healthy, they were likely to be drafted into military service and forced to fight (and kill) in a war many felt was illegal and immoral. In total, over fifteen million military college deferments were granted during the Vietnam War era.

Yet even the deferments students obtained from Hiram Scott, as well as thousands of other colleges and universities during that period, were in many cases only temporary reprieves from what I define as fate, but what could also be defined as luck, divine intervention, or simply being in the wrong place at the wrong time.

The irony was many characters in my story would have been, in retrospect, safer going to Vietnam than pursuing a higher education in Western Nebraska. For them, timing was everything, and fate, it seems, will in the end have its way with all of us.

Like Jon, the protagonist in my story, I traveled back to Scottsbluff several years ago, looking for something. Closure? Also, like Jon, I found the town to be as picturesque and as welcoming as it was when I was there so many years ago. But my visit also conjured up devastating memories of lost friends and the idiocy of an insane war.

I also revisited a place where good times were had, lots of beer consumed, and my visit made me laugh out loud remembering things that can only occur when you are nineteen years old and living in a dorm with some crazy guys who had more money than common sense. Yeah, what could go wrong with that combination?

Clearly, the backdrop of my year in Nebraska was the Vietnam War. But for some reason, in that fleeting period of time of the mid-sixties, the war seemed to be farther away, as if we had escaped its grasp, or it had forgotten all about us living in the wilds of Nebraska while we drank beer, played basketball, and did what college students do. But that feeling was short-lived, and we all knew that the reality was we were deluding ourselves, and the war would eventually catch up with all of us, one way or the other. And it did.

We all knew other young men who went to Vietnam and never came back, and their headstones in our local cemeteries bear witness to that unarguable and inescapable fact. Many who did come home were permanently damaged physically, mentally, or emotionally, but all of us who lived during that period were, in one way or another, affected by a war that seems more and more senseless as the years pass.

It's been almost fifty years since the Vietnam War ended, and for younger generations, it is nothing more than just another chapter in American history. So perhaps the best way to understand that era is to listen to some of the cool music that helped define those years and the generation who lived through it. Songs like Phil Ochs' "What Are You Fighting For," Barry McGuire's "Eve of Destruction," Country Joe and the Fish's "I Feel Like I'm Fixin' to Die," Marvin Gaye's anthem "What's Goin On," or films like *Platoon, Coming Home, Born on the Fourth of July,* among so many others, all tell the story of that era far better than any history book.

From a personal perspective I NEEDED to write this book. Years of thinking back to those days are testament to the impact that year in Scottsbluff had on my life. In short, it was a story that had taken up residence in my brain since 1966. So, here it is.

For you strict historians, remember literary license is a real thing, and for you fiction lovers, you can try to figure out what is fact and what are my personal brain droppings.

I'll never tell.

Mark Donahue

Dateline: Chicago Tribune

Re: Final Edition/Heading West

May 22, 2016

Dear Loyal Readers,

When you're seventeen, you think you have it all figured out. In your still developing, naivete-addled mind, the future is clear: step one will lead to step two, and all you must do is follow each carefully orchestrated step. Things will turn out the way you want, according to *your* plan, the way everything is supposed to be.

After all, what could possibly go wrong? But then something does go wrong, and as an old Yiddish saying goes, "Man plans, and God laughs."

While I must admit, I have my doubts about all that God stuff, I do wonder sometimes if there are forces at work that we can't see, can't control, as if someone or something had another plan in mind for us. It is almost like things were put in place when we were born, and while we might take a circuitous route, we will inevitably be led back to where we are supposed to be no matter how we fight and claw to stay on our personally plotted course.

Obviously, not everyone creates a plan for their life. Instead, they react to what occurs on a day-to-day basis and take whatever comes their way. I have often wondered if the non-planners might have the right idea. That group seems to freelance or ad-lib life, and sometimes that appears to work out just fine. Of course, other times, it's clear that a lack of planning can lead to less than desirable outcomes regarding the life game.

As this will be my final article at this august and venerable newspaper, I wanted to give you, my readers and friends, a general idea of what I'll be doing over the next few years just so you don't think I'll be going off into the sunset with no plan in mind and spending my days chugging Budweisers and picking lint from my navel, although the former may occur more times than the latter.

See, even now, I have a plan, but what I don't know is whether someone else also has a plan for me that is, well, different from mine, which could lead me to something far afield from what I have in mind today as I write these words.

So, here's the deal. I do have a general idea of what I *think* I want to do with the rest of my life, which begins in a few days with me heading west on I-80. But I promise myself and you guys that I'll be flexible. I will also write down my new experiences and some of my old memories in what I will call a journal, although I was never quite sure how a journal differed from a diary, but I digress. Whatever I write I will someday share with you guys depending on how embarrassing, ridiculous, or even slightly illegal some of those things might be … if you promise not to tell anyone else.

See, one thing I've learned over the years is that fighting those unseen forces I mentioned above that seem to control our lives can cause problems and wastes time, a valuable and diminishing commodity that I no longer have in abundance. I have grudgingly come to realize and accept I am in fact "circling the drain," but before I head inevitably downward in a tighter and tighter spiral, I want to revisit some things. Things that I have never forgotten. Look for people I have missed. And search for a time in my life I still think and dream about.

Those of us who lived through the '60s and '70s will never forget those times, even though there are some memories that are painful to recall, and in my case, they will probably be even more painful to revisit.

But I am committed to this Quixotic adventure and look forward to what will come next in my life, although I have no idea how or where my story will end. Of course, that is my plan. What I am not sure of is if *my* plan will pan out or if someone else's will win the day in the end.

Thanks for everything, dear readers. You have been very kind to me over the years. Stay tuned for … something.

Your friend,

Jon ("JT") Taylor

Chapter 1

San Diego: 1964

Seventeen-year-old Jon sat with his parents at the family dining room table and ate spaghetti with homemade meatballs while they watched Walter Cronkite deliver the evening news on CBS. The black-and-white images showed thousands of students participating in an anti-war march in Washington, DC.

Jon's father, Paul, a veteran of WWII, was not amused. "Those long-haired punks need to get a shower, a haircut, and get their asses a job rather than doing all that marching and raising hell."

"I think they're marching because they're afraid the war might expand and lots more boys might get killed over there," Jon's mother, Doris, speculated as she passed around the warm Italian garlic bread.

Tearing off a piece of the bread, Paul reasoned, "Better to fight those communists over there than here."

"A few guys in my class have already enlisted in the army," Jon said absentmindedly as he read *Sports Illustrated* between large bites of tossed salad with vinegar and oil dressing.

"That'll be a great experience for those boys, teach them how to be men," Paul proclaimed.

"Getting shot is not really a great experience. Besides, you always said how much you hated the army," Doris reminded him.

"Sure, some of the stuff was bad, but we were doing our duty and protecting our country."

"My history teacher said Vietnam could be like quicksand, and the U.S. could get sucked into something pretty bad," Jon interjected as he was skimming an article about the upcoming Major League Baseball season.

"Bet your history teacher has long hair and needs a bath."

"Never noticed he needed a bath, but his hair is kind of long," Jon admitted.

"See, that little skirmish over there will be over in a couple months. You really think a crappy little country like Vietnam could stand up to the United States of America?" Paul reasoned, recognizing the utter invincibility of the U.S. military and sheer genius of America's political leadership.

JT — My dad did have a point. After I finally found Vietnam on a map, the country was to be sure very small, and the idea that it could somehow defeat the U.S. in any kind of war seemed preposterous.

I also questioned how serious it really was over in Vietnam when the newspapers and TV guys kept calling it a "police action." That sounded like a term I had read in my history books about the Korean War (or conflict) back in the early '50s. After all, how could a police action or conflict grow into some kind of real war where tons of guys could be killed? But then I vaguely remembered my American History teacher, Mr. Brown, telling us America had not really won the Korean War and instead had agreed to an armistice.

He had called it America's Forgotten War. I wasn't sure what he had meant by that at the time. And truthfully, I didn't really care since I had, in fact, forgotten about that little war and was more concerned how the Anaheim Angels were going to do that year in the American League West.

Sure, some guys had died over in Vietnam as early as 1962. But a few dozen dead guys did not seem all that many. Even the next year, when more than twice that many were killed, it seemed a small price to pay for our freedom; at least that's what my friend Bobby's father said during a quarter-limit poker night at our house one evening in 1963. Of course, they did not know any of the families who had lost a son. But that would change.

I remember in 1963 and 1964, the press, in general, began to give the ever-increasing number of peace marches and the college campus unrest some coverage. The so-called "limited conflict in Southeast Asia" also gained some airtime on the national TV networks' evening newscasts. This included Walter Cronkite on CBS, Huntley-Brinkley on NBC, and Ron Cochran on ABC. But what was happening thousands of miles away seldom was the lead story on national TV news broadcasts, or national magazines like *Time*, *The Saturday Evening Post*, or *Newsweek*. The local news coverage was even less.

The exception to limited local media coverage was when a neighborhood soldier was killed in the "conflict." While national print coverage was increasing in *The New York Times*, *LA Times*, *Chicago Tribune*, and *The Wall Street Journal*, it was hardly a cover story or front-page news, even though the American death toll had risen from fifty-three killed in 1962 to 122 in 1963 and would grow to 216 in 1964.

Yet, when 126,348 Americans died in car crashes and over three hundred died by lightning strikes over the same period, it seemed like a small price to pay to "keep the commies at bay" thousands of miles away. The war was sneaking up on all of us, and when we finally saw the monster heading our way, it would be too late.

Chapter 2

Vietnam: 1964

A putrid, yellow-tinged haze hung over the rice paddy nearly twenty-four hours after the combat had ended. The ninety-four-degree temperature and ninety percent humidity mixed with rotting flesh, jungle mold, and blood-soaked grasses to create a noxious stench that made breathing labored and vomit-inducing.

Throughout the previous night, the sounds of the dying had gone silent. What hours before had been whimpering prayers in English and Vietnamese had ceased, and what remained were the caws of hundreds of birds that pecked at the decaying bodies. The raptors had little preference on which nationality they feasted. Any body would do.

In a patch of elephant grass near a pile of dead Viet Cong, two eighteen-year-old US Army PFCs from San Diego, Bobby and Gary, lay side by side on their backs with their heads nearly touching. They peered up at the gathering clouds, which would soon produce another of the never-ending downpours that invaded the area every day around 3 p.m. "That one looks like a dog," Bobby said in a labored whisper.

"A dog? You crazy, man? That looks like an airplane," Gary replied, not really seeing an airplane or a dog, given the shrapnel fragments that had entered his skull the night before and partially blinded him.

But Bobby kept on seeing things. "See the one next to it? It looks like a school bus."

"Oh yeah, I can see that for sure. Looks like the one we used to ride in Cali when we were kids," Gary kind of remembered.

"Yeah, it does. I remember seeing Marsha Howe on that bus every day. What a fucking body."

"Oh yeah, I remember her, hot blonde with nice tits. I think she dug me," Gary clearly remembered.

"Are you fucking crazy? She never knew you and I even existed."

"Bullshit, she smiled at me all the time."

"She smiled at everybody, you fucking idiot," Bobby whispered, his voice weaker by the moment.

"Yeah, but I'm not the fucking moron who had the great idea we should enlist in the fucking army."

"We would've been drafted sooner or later," Bobby countered as he looked down and saw beetles, flies, worms, and other assorted fauna devouring the shredded remains of his left leg. He casually wondered why the sight of his torn flesh being consumed by the local wildlife was not more physically painful or emotionally disturbing to him. He figured it was because at that moment he no longer gave a flying fuck about much of anything.

But he did wonder if his childhood buddy lying next to him, still looking at the clouds, realized that both of his legs were gone below the knee and lay six feet away under a bush. He thought it might be impolite to raise that issue.

"Hey, remember the time we skipped school … went surfing, and met those girls from LA?" Gary asked.

"Fuckin' A, and they were worth getting detention for. Wonder what those girls are doing this minute and if they remember us."

"Hell, yes, they remember us. They're probably laying out on the beach and looking for us right now. That was a fun day … but it seems like a hundred years ago."

"Yeah, but it's only been five months," Bobby said.

After several more minutes of silence, Gary asked in an almost impatient tone, "You 'bout ready to go?"

"Yeah, just give me another minute," Bobby whispered.

"Why, you wanna comb your damn hair to try and look pretty?"

"Fuck you, shit for brains. You know, if you hadn't stepped on that fucking mine, we wouldn't be …"

"Look around, asshole. We'd be dead anyway," Gary reminded his best friend and former Little League teammate.

Bobby did his best to shift his view and look around. What he saw were the remains of what looked like over one hundred Viet Cong, mostly under eighteen years old, scattered in pieces over the matted, grassy landscape. Among those remains, he also saw the bodies, or pieces of bodies, of what he guessed to be over thirty dead American soldiers lying in what was now a deluge of rain. "Yeah, I guess you're right. Guess we were pretty fucked either way."

"Yeah, we were fucked all right," Gary said softly.

In the distance, the shredded teenage soldiers could hear the *whomp, whomp, whomp* of at least two Bell UH-1 (Huey) helicopters approaching from the south.

"Should we wait?" Bobby asked.

"Wait? Fuck no, I ain't goin' home and facing everybody lookin' like this. C'mon, let's do this shit."

"Are you sure, Gary?"

"Yeah, I'm real sure, but not the head. People won't be able to recognize us."

"Good thinking for a fucking idiot."

"Fuck you. And by the way, Marsha Howe did smile at me; at least I really think she did."

Bobby painfully turned his head and looked over at Gary, smiled, then said, "Yeah, I remember now, she for sure smiled at you. Yeah, she dug you, man."

Gary returned the smile as he and Bobby pulled out their Colt 1911s, linked arms, and placed the barrels against their chests. "On three?" Gary whispered.

"Yeah, on three, and don't fuck me over and chicken out."

"I told you, you've already been royally fucked over, big boy."

In unison, the young men counted to three. Neither chickened out.

Chapter 3

Scottsbluff, Nebraska
A College Would Be Nice: 1964

Broadway was the two-lane main drag that ran through downtown Scottsbluff. It featured nearly all of the businesses in town, including Western Auto, JCPenney, Vic's Pizza, a feed store, several clothing establishments, a jewelry store, and the Midwest Theater, which played mostly year-old releases from Hollywood. It also had a diner, a bakery, three taverns, a drugstore, a TV repair shop, an out-of-business furniture store, and the Lincoln Hotel, which proudly displayed on a bronze plaque that it was constructed in 1919.

The city's municipal building was a redbrick, two-story structure with not one but two American flags on rusted metal poles that were erected after World Wars I and II. Each also had a bronze plaque at its base listing the names of the local dead and missing who had served their country in times of war. Each spring, women from the local military auxiliary would plant poppies of various colors to honor the dead, who few living local citizens remembered.

In a poorly lit, smoke-filled room adorned with two buffalo heads on a recently painted beige wall, next to yet another huge American flag, the city treasurer, a tall, slender woman named Betty, cleared her throat in anticipation of making her annual financial presentation to the mayor and city council.

In preparation for the event, she had purchased a new but shapeless yellow-green printed dress from a used clothing store that she felt complemented her straight brown hair and horn-rimmed glasses. She addressed the five-man council and the three-term mayor in a dull monotone while she delivered a dire financial report on the "State of Scottsbluff."

"At the current spending rates, we'll run out of cash in late May of this year. As a result, it will be necessary to increase property taxes and perhaps implement both a 1 percent city and county sales tax to avoid insolvency and meet our financial obligations for the next thirty-six months."

Not waiting for comment, Betty returned to her seat next to the mayor and faced the five city council members, who all wore short-sleeve white shirts and thin black ties and puffed on Lucky Strikes.

After silently digesting Betty's less-than-rosy financial report, the mayor finally spoke up. "Well, that's a hell of a thing. You mean, the whole damn city is broke?"

"Yes, sir, Mr. Mayor. We're broke flatter than hell," Betty confirmed in her consistent, definitive, and never-wavering monotone.

Buck, a feed store owner and veteran of fifteen years on the city council, had an immediate observation. "If we start raising taxes now, we'll get our asses thrown out come November."

Earl, the local undertaker, had an idea. "Then we should announce the tax hikes in December."

"Then we'll get shot in January," the mayor chimed in with the clear-thinking certainty of an experienced Nebraska politician who was aware of the percentage of gun owners in Scottsbluff.

Harold, the local Allstate Insurance agent, had a solid suggestion. "We need to give this some serious thought. Let's go over to Hight's, get some beers and burgers, and talk this thing over."

Irwin, a retired pharmacist, had a fiscal question. "Can the city afford burgers and beers?"

Ignoring Irwin's semi-sarcastic question, Jerry, the owner of the local John Deere tractor franchise, said, "What we need are more farmers around here."

"C'mon, Jerry, this is 1964, not 1864," the mayor reminded.

Hight's Bar and Grill had been around since the 1930s, and while new ownership had changed the menus from time to time, they never seemed to buy new tables or chairs, change the yellowed pictures on the walls, or clean out the bugs that accumulated in the bottom of the overhead light fixtures. What they did provide was cold beer, excellent burgers and fries, and, on the weekends, outstanding fried chicken served with macaroni and cheese, topped off with homemade apple pie and ice cream.

After finishing off their burgers and fries, along with three pitchers of Miller High Life, the mayor, the five council members, and Betty had run out of serious thoughts and any novel ideas on how to avoid financial calamity in Scottsbluff without all of them being tossed out of their jobs after the next election. This was aside from Jerry's repeated mantra that agriculture in some form and the requisite new farmers were the key to the long-term success of the community. The rest of the group ignored Jerry, who ignored being ignored.

"This town is dyin' on the vine. No new businesses, no new money, no new ideas, just the same damn thing every year—beets and sugar—while the costs for fixin' the roads and sidewalks and teachers' salaries keep goin' up," Harold said.

Buck added, "Yep, when our kids leave high school, they run off to the big cities like Casper, Lincoln, and Omaha and never come back."

"You blame 'em? Hell, we stayed around here, and look at us," the mayor accurately observed.

After ordering a fourth pitcher of beer, the group revisited the problems in Scottsbluff. "This town needs some good jobs so all the kids don't leave after high school," Buck said.

"Hell, *we* need good jobs so we don't leave," Harold added as he looked up at the wall-mounted black-and-white TV, where Walter Cronkite was describing an anti-war march in Washington, DC.

"Hey, Harold, where the hell is that Vietnam place? I ain't never heard of it," Buck asked, between sips of Miller High Life.

After hearing Walter's "and that's the way it is" sign-off, and chowing down on his second chili dog, Harold said, "I think it's so close to Japan, you could probably walk it."

"Look at all those draft-dodgin' college kids marching. Wonder where they come from?" Irwin asked as he, too, glanced up at the TV.

"They come from places just like Scottsbluff," the mayor informed.

The entire group stared at the TV in silence for over a minute. Then Betty had an epiphany, albeit one she shared in her usual monotone. "The way we get kids to stay home is to have a college right here in Scottsbluff. That way, after they graduate, they won't have any need to leave town since they could start their own businesses right here, make some money, and create new jobs. That would bring in tax revenue, not to mention all the tuition dollars that would flow into town."

After a few moments of reflective silence, several of the commissioners laughed at Betty's suggestion.

"Don't laugh, I'm dead serious. We need a college right here in Scottsbluff," Betty insisted, refusing to deviate from her monotone or be intimidated by men her father's age.

"Betty, you can't just start a damn college. That takes big money," Harold stated, taking on the voice of reason with a touch of finality.

"It does happen infrequently, but Harold is right on this one, Betty. Colleges take big money," Irwin said in a tone with even more finality as if the subject was closed.

Betty was in no mood to close the subject. "We all know there's investment money available in this county if people think it'll mean new jobs and new opportunities for growth. It'd be a kind of economic development project that maybe taxpayers might get behind even if we had to raise taxes a little."

"You know, Betty might be right. Today, kids' parents do pay big bucks to send their little Johnny off to college so he doesn't get his ass shot off in places like Vietnam," Harold said.

"Plus, the students and faculty will need places to live; they'll go to restaurants, buy gas, food, clothes. They'll go to bars, Jim's Carryout; they all drink like fish. They'll go to laundromats, to doctors, dentists, and barbershops," Betty said in what for her was a flourish of unbridled and even passionate emotion.

For several minutes the rest of the council sat in silence as they sipped beer and munched on the cold French fries that remained in paper-lined red plastic baskets. They tried their best to intellectually digest the new idea that had been proffered and now expanded on by Betty, who was, after all, a bookkeeper, so she had to understand the numbers.

From time to time, they also looked up at the black-and-white TV and saw all those marching long-haired college students carrying signs. Finally, they looked back at each other.

"Maybe you have something there, Betty. You know, I think we could have a college up and running in a year or so if we can raise some local cash," Buck said.

"I guess a college might work, but who'd come to Scottsbluff, Nebraska?" Irwin asked.

Pointing to the TV, Betty said, "All those college boys who want deferments to stay out of the draft would be a good place to start. They'll want to get into any college. Even a brand-new one in Scottsbluff, Nebraska. Bring the boys here, and the girls will follow."

"I think we just need to recruit, you know, more farmers from other towns," Jerry insisted as he finished off the fries. "Besides, I don't think this town should in any way create a place that will attract some damn draft dodgers. It ain't American."

"What if the students were farmer wannabe-type draft dodgers, Jerry? Would that be okay with you?" Betty asked.

Stuck for an answer to that complex socioeconomic-political question, Jerry demurred and ordered more fries up at the bar.

Finally, it was the mayor who clarified and moved the clever and creative college idea forward. "You know, I never said anything to you guys before, but I actually had that very idea of starting a college here at least a year ago, maybe two. I just didn't want to tell you guys or anybody else about it until I had time to thoroughly research and study the whole issue in minute detail, which I have now done. And if you guys agree with my idea of a college right here in town, I think I could put the strong arm on a dozen business guys here in Scottsbluff to come up with some cash to fund the start-up. I'll bet we could use some of the old, abandoned buildings down on Broadway, like Smith's Furniture store, for classrooms."

"We could use the Lincoln Hotel for a dorm until some are built. That place hasn't been full in thirty years," Buck added.

"Great minds, Buck. That was part of my plan too," the mayor said.

Over the next hour, and fueled by more Miller High Life, the city council began to buy into the mayor's great idea mainly because they did not have many other viable options.

They agreed starting a new college carried some significant financial risks, but even if the college failed down the road, it would generate some immediate excitement. In addition to bringing in a badly needed cash infusion to the community, a college could maybe even grow the town's image and visibility, which could be enhanced even more if the college fielded football and basketball teams that would bring attention to the school, act as a recruiting tool, and most importantly be a source of ticket sales.

The football and basketball idea came from Betty, although the mayor said he had already also thought of that as part of his now three-year-old mental college plan … which he never shared with anyone until that very night.

"What are we gonna call this college?" Buck asked the mayor, who undoubtedly had an answer since he alone had thought up the entire college idea.

"How about Hiram Scott College, after that trapper guy?" the mayor suggested.

"Great idea, Mr. Mayor. Wow, you sure are on a roll tonight with some great ideas," Harold said.

"Thanks. Like I said I've been thinking about this college thing for over three years now."

As the group filed out of Hight's, bubbling over with enthusiasm over the mayor's truly creative and borderline brilliant ideas to save the town from financial ruin, he smiled warmly and held the door for Betty. She stopped, turned to him, and whispered with a smile, "Mr. Mayor, you can go fuck yourself tonight, because I most certainly will not. Not tonight, not ever again. *Ever.* You're also a fucking asshole. And I quit."

CHAPTER 4

SAN DIEGO FUNERAL HOME: 1964

The incongruous juxtaposition of a funeral home being across the street from a beach where beautiful young people surfed, played volleyball, and made out on cotton blankets was seemingly lost on the long line of mourners who attended the funerals of two other beautiful young people who only months before had played on that same stretch of beach.

Their open caskets were only made possible because one of the boys had, in a moment of clarity and fueled by Southern Californian surfer vanity, suggested that, given their horrific wounds, he and his best friend each take a slug in their hearts rather than blowing their heads off and most certainly messing up their handsome faces.

> JT — The one thing I vividly remember about that night in the funeral home was the smell. I can't say it smelled bad; it was just a weird smell. Like someone had sprayed too much Lysol to hide the smell of something, and then sprayed something else to hide the smell of the Lysol. Maybe I thought it smelled like dead people. That was a guess since I had never knowingly smelled a dead person before. However, I did, without question, detect a lot of English Leather aftershave in the air that night too.

The attendees of the funeral for the two local boys, Gary and Bobby, were an eclectic amalgam of former high school friends, relatives, the morbidly curious, and members of the military, who wore full-dress uniforms just like the ones the best friends wore in their caskets.

> JT — Next to each casket was an American flag with an alive army soldier who stood vigil. I remember wondering if those currently

alive soldiers were at all concerned about eventually being dead soldiers or if that thought ever entered their brains.

I was later told by a friend of mine who worked at the funeral home that Bobby and Gary had set a world record for embalming fluid used to keep them from completely wasting away prior to their open casket viewings. This was the result of it taking over two weeks to transfer them in body bags from the frontline to a temporary mortuary in Saigon, to a military mortuary in San Diego after a seventeen-hour flight, and finally to the local funeral home, where the mortician tried his best to hide the grievous injuries to both young men and make their faces look as close as possible to the high school yearbook photos that were placed on tables next to each coffin. That task was made all the harder by the fact the boys had in life been All-American, blond surfer types, which, despite best efforts, was not what we saw in the caskets.

Since Gary and Bobby were best friends who had grown up together in San Diego, enlisted in the army together, and after only five months in Vietnam died together in the jungle muck, it was decided by someone that it was only altogether proper and fitting that they should share a funeral and be buried side by side at a local cemetery. I always figured they would have been okay with that decision.

People lined up in the funeral home and walked down a flower-lined aisleway with a casket on either side. This configuration saved time and kept the lines moving as it seemed no one wanted to linger given how both bodies, especially the faces, which had thick paste makeup and red lips, seemed … not right. The bodies, as to be expected, were rigid, which made it appear the guys were at some kind of afterlife attention.

Their faces looked not at all like the handsome, tanned teenagers who had left for Vietnam only months before on an "adventure."

JT — When I looked down at the guys as I walked past their coffins, I thought I detected the slightest grin on Bobby's face, like he wasn't really dead at all and this whole funeral thing was a big joke. I half expected him to sit up at any moment and say, "Suckerrrrs, I fooled your asses." That was his favorite line. But I knew that was not going to happen, as Bobby and Gary were dead as hell, and I kept wondering

… why? What had been gained by their deaths? Was America safer? Was communism finally in check and we could sleep better with Gary and Bobby dead and buried? The idea of never seeing the guys again came over me like a wave as I looked at their distorted faces, which despite the best efforts of the morticians looked nothing like the guys I had known.

Beach Boys' music played during the service. This was much to the dismay of the older veterans who attended but was at the request of the dead soldiers' mothers, who, under the circumstances, got their way as to what was appropriate musical accompaniment for two dead nineteen-year-olds who were best buddies, former surfers, baseball infielders, and guitar players.

Some of our former classmates and baseball teammates of Gary and Bobby walked past their coffins in silence. After giving their condolences to both families, they lingered in the funeral home even after the minister had made comments about how brave the guys had been and what heroes they were, although he did not detail what their specific acts of heroism were other than being two dead guys.

The minister also talked about how they had been best friends and how they would now be in heaven together.

"If they're in heaven together, they're probably trying to get laid," Tom whispered to his friend Chris.

"I heard each of their legs had been shot off," Matthew said.

"Why the fuck did those dumb asses quit school and go to Vietnam?" Patrick asked.

"Remember that army recruiter who came to school last spring? Gary said that guy told him he could become an officer and retire when he was forty. Both guys were gung-ho about being soldiers and really believed the war over there is a good thing. They bought into all that patriotic bullshit, so they dropped out of school and enlisted," Chris whispered.

Despite getting the side-eye from some people sitting around them for their whispered conversation, the guys kept it up.

"Gary was a cool guy, but let's face it, he wasn't the brightest bulb in the pack," Phillip said, not cruelly but accurately.

"Neither was Bobby. But they were pretty cool guys. They loved the Beach Boys, and Gary was a good singer," Robert remembered.

"I wonder if they got shot and died right away or if it took a while for them to die. I heard both had their arms shot off," Patrick offered.

"No, it was their legs, all four of their legs were blown to shit," Phillip clarified.

"You guys are gross," Jon's girlfriend, Valerie, said to the rest of the group after overhearing their conversations.

"Not gross, just curious as to the specifics of the demise of our former teammates," Jon clarified.

JT — I hated it, but Valerie and I had been nicknamed Barbie and Ken by the rest of our junior class. Further, it was assumed that when I graduated from one of the military academies that I had been recommended to by a local senator friend of my dad, I would end up as a general or admiral, and then after a few years of serving my country, I would go to Yale grad school and follow my first love of being a writer. I would then work at *The New York Times* or *Washington Post* and win a couple of Pulitzers. I had solid plans.

The story also went that Valerie and I would come back to Hollywood, and I would write novels or scripts or both, and we would end up living on the beach in Malibu. Another good plan. In fact, it was a great fucking plan.

Valerie, on the other hand, would end up doing whatever beautiful, wealthy young women do when their hardworking husbands make a shitload of money before they are thirty. But it was agreed that she would likely try to star in one of my films.

Everyone agreed Jon's girlfriend, Val, was superhot with a killer body and had selected Jon in seventh grade to be her breeding partner, although Jon was unaware of Valerie's decision. Val saw in Jon not only good looks but also talent, brains, and the kind of money-making potential that was worthy of her fucking his brains out in high school to ensure his return from whatever academy or Ivy League school he attended. That was *her* plan.

JT — Despite the bad taste jokes the guys were cracking about our newly dead former classmates, it was the first time any of us had actually seen a dead person outside of one of our grandparents who was supposed to die. Bobby and Gary weren't supposed to die, not at eighteen years old in a smelly Vietnam swamp.

Seeing them lying there in their coffins, looking pasty and stiff, unnerved us—all of us—although no one would admit it and instead used dead-person humor to hide how we really felt, which was sad, scared, and unsure … about everything.

Only months before, we were all joking with Gary and Bobby about why they had enlisted, but neither of them seemed worried about the possibility that they might return home in pieces inside body bags.

It seemed as if both of them saw Vietnam as a kind of patriotic adventure that they were both excited about. That excitement lasted five months and ended when their hearts were exploded in their chests by their army-issue pistols, in the pouring rain, eight thousand miles from home, surrounded by scores of other dead young men who had been called on by their respective governments to kill. They did as ordered.

"You should see the rifles we'll be firing. They're cool as hell," Bobby had said.

"Yeah, we have a contest on who will kill the most commies," Gary added.

Knowing Gary and Bobby as I did, I never really believed they were the type of guys who would kill anyone, much less become famous for setting records for indiscriminate murder, even in a time of war. But I learned later that the army had the ability to create killing machines out of otherwise peaceful and even gentle baseball players and high school cutups. I remember hoping that had not happened to Gary and Bobby.

While we all continued with the sick dead jokes until the ceremony was over, much to the chagrin of our girlfriends, it was all a show. Seeing Bobby and Gary hit all of us in a way none of us ever expected.

The war that had been a page-five story in the local papers had now come home to San Diego as it had to an increasing number of cities across the country.

Everyone at the funeral home had known and liked Gary and Bobby, and now they were really, totally, and irretrievably dead, and the dead classmates humor wasn't as funny as the guys were pretending it to be.

As people filed out of the funeral home after the ceremony, they each stopped to give final condolences to the parents of the dead boys. Gary's mom, a small blonde in her early forties, appeared in a daze as she robotically shook hands and nodded, accepting the sympathies from those who shook her hand.

JT — I remember how weird I felt when Valerie and I gave our condolences to Gary's mom and dad, whom I knew very well. I mean, what can you say in a situation like that? Nothing could bring Gary back. Nothing you could say would make them feel better. Nothing could make them feel less hurt and pain. For some reason, I felt guilty for being alive.

His parents were neat people. It was a close-knit family, and I used to stay over there every Friday night. We'd make homemade Chef Boyardee pizzas, drink a ton of Pepsi, and watch *Twilight Zone* and *77 Sunset Strip*. His mom would always make us a big breakfast on Saturday mornings, and his dad would play basketball with us on the weekends. It was a cool family.

A week after the funeral, Gary's mom put a pistol in her mouth, pulled the trigger, and sprayed her brains all over her recently remodeled kitchen. Later that day, her husband came from work, discovered his wife on the floor, picked up the pistol, and shot himself in his right temple. It had been less than a year since my last pizza/*Twilight Zone* sleepover at Gary's house. It seemed way longer.

CHAPTER 5

SAN DIEGO LOVER'S LANE: 1964

The radio on Jon's 1957 Ford convertible played Barbara Mason's "Yes, I'm Ready" as Jon and Valerie made out under a June full moon overlooking the Pacific Ocean while a warm breeze enveloped the half-dressed couple.

Jon was still basking in the fact he had received notification of his pending appointment to the Naval Academy, which meant his education would be free, a fact that greatly pleased his father on many levels, mostly financial.

Jon had even garnered financial support from some wealthy members of his church, identifying him as someone "whose deep religious beliefs, academic record, athletic achievements, along with his ethical, personal, moral standards, and his community involvement, were attributes worthy of financial support from our church members to attend one of the nation's most prestigious universities." The church scholarship was to pay for "extras" during Jon's stay at Annapolis.

JT — The hard, cold reality back then was I was not a particularly religious guy. Even now, I guess I'm still looking for some proof. It's just that organized religion seems like so much hypocritical bullshit to me. Always did. The older I get, the more proof I want.

To be honest, the only reason I attended the church at all growing up back then was my father had heard of the annual scholarships that were awarded and told me as early as sixth grade to get my ass to church, keep my grades up, and maybe I would be able to attend one of the military academies or an Ivy League school some day because there was no way in fucking hell my family could afford such a thing.

Truth be known, I was not crazy about going to the Naval Academy except, of course, for that free education thing, and if that idiot war got out of hand in Vietnam and a military draft was instituted, I would already be in the service as an officer. Far better to get a Bachelor of Science degree from Annapolis than being a marine crawling around on a jungle floor when, rumor had it, a person could conceivably get his legs blown off.

While mindful of the requirement to serve at least five years in the navy after graduation, Jon surmised he could make that time pass by working on the various novels he had floating around in his brain and then, after his five years were up, he would apply to Harvard, Yale, or Princeton and pursue the writing career he had always aspired to.

The bottom line was the Naval Academy was a means to an end for Jon, driven by economics and not patriotism, especially when the country was engaged in a war that he thought was totally asinine. At the same time, he had noticed how women reacted to men in naval uniforms, and in case things didn't work out with Valerie, he would be increasing his chances in the world of romance.

On hearing of the academy acceptance and financial aid, Valerie was far less excited over the news than Jon thought she would be. Or should be. She also demonstrated a decided lack of geographical comprehension when she said, "Oh, Jonny, I am going to miss you so much next year, when you are off to college. New York is so far away."

"Actually, the Naval Academy is in Maryland, babe. And I'll miss you too, but you can come visit, and I'll be home for the holidays."

Later, while Valerie moved her head up and down in his lap, Jon stared out over the Pacific and wondered what the next few years would bring in terms of intellectual growth and ultimately development of his writing skills at an Ivy League school. He thought about the kinds of interesting people he would meet and what lay ahead after college. His thoughts were interrupted by a question from Valerie, who looked up at him and asked, "Do you like this, Jonny?"

After a hoarse, "Yeah, this is great," Jon pushed Valerie's head back into his lap.

A few moments later, Valerie rose again with an announcement. "I got the pill."

"What?"

"My mom got me the pill, so we can do the real thing now."

"Oh, that's great, but this is fine, really," Jon said as he again *encouraged* Valerie's head downward.

But like the Phoenix, Valerie rose yet again and said, "Jonny, I want the first time to be with you. I'm afraid you'll go off to college and I'll never see you again, and New York is so far away."

"Like I said, babe, I'll be in Maryland and …"

"I guess that's closer, but it's still really far away."

"Well, actually, no, it isn't …"

"Jonny, I really love you, and I want the first time to be with you, now, tonight."

"Yeah, but those pills don't always work and …"

"Yes, they do. They always work. I want to feel you inside me and for us to be together, always."

"I think we should wait and …"

At that moment Valerie slowly sat up, unbuttoned her Villager blouse, and proudly displayed her 34-C lace bra, before she languidly unhooked it from the back and sat in silence with a small but noticeable and knowing smile on her face, waiting for Jon to respond as she was pretty sure he would.

After several more moments of looking deep into Jon's green eyes while his green eyes looked deeply into her 34-C's, she said in a whisper, "Don't you want me like I want you, Jonny?"

JT — In a matter of seconds, I had totally and completely compartmentalized and analyzed the entire situation before me. I used what I knew of the scientific method and surmised that Valerie was absolutely … probably … most likely correct in her knowledge of the pill based on what, I was certain, had been her deep and thorough research into birth control usage. I was also certain that medical science had, in fact, perfected the birth control pill so that it worked each and every time. No exceptions.

At a base level, I also concluded that Valerie had exceptionally great tits, and if I did not, in fact, fuck her on that very perfect, star-lit, California night, with Johnny Mathis on the radio, I would regret it the rest of my life. So, I did.

And I did.

Four months later, Jon was sitting in the high school library, preparing for a physics test when Valerie sat down across from him. "We need to talk," she said in a whisper.

Jon did not look up from his book. "I have a test later, and I need to study."

Valerie leaned closer, and whispered louder, "I'm late."

Jon still did not look up. "For what?"

"You know … late."

Finally, Jon looked up from a chapter in his physics book titled Vectors and Projectiles and stared at Valerie for several moments. "You mean …?"

"Looks like I'm due in March."

"What the hell happened?" Jon said in a voice that sounded like a gasp.

"I think maybe the pill fell out."

"You mean you put the pill in …?"

"Don't pick on me, it was all your fault anyway, you forced me, I didn't want to do it, you know I wanted to wait."

"What?! How about the last four months? You mean I forced you every night?"

"We can talk later; I need to get to class," Valerie said before she walked off in a huff.

JT — As I watched Valerie walk away, I remember sitting there in the library in a semi-daze for several minutes even after the bell rang.

I intuitively knew that from that moment on, my precisely planned-out future had changed. Maybe not a change I would recognize the next day, week, or month, but without question, everything that was going to be was now *not* going to be. My life's plan was going to be different, and I had no one to blame but myself.

Two weeks later, Jon sat at the kitchen table with NBC's Huntley and Brinkley in the background and relayed bad news to his parents. "I got a letter from the Naval Academy rescinding my appointment because of an 'ethics violation' on my part. The church also called and said they have taken back their scholarship offer because of …"

His father put down the evening paper, stopped chewing his macaroni and cheese, and stared over the top of the business section. "Dammit, I knew that would happen. How did Annapolis find out?"

"Not sure, but I know Valerie has told some of her friends she is pregnant, so I guess word leaked out."

"What the hell were you thinking? I told you to keep it in your pants."

His mother immediately went into alternative mode. "What about USC or UCLA?" All the while understanding that his father had not kept it in his pants either.

"I called them, but they already gave out all their scholarships and have a waiting list a mile long of all the guys wanting to get in this year because of the damn war."

"If you don't get in somewhere, you're gonna get your ass drafted," his father said.

"I know, so I applied here and got accepted already," Jon said and handed his parents a brochure.

"What the hell is Hiram Scott?" his father asked.

"It's a new college in Scottsbluff, Nebraska."

"Where?" his mother inquired.

"Nebraska. I can go there for a year and then transfer."

"Well, it's not Harvard, but it's not Hanoi either," his mother accurately noted.

CHAPTER 6

TRENTON, NEW JERSEY: MARCH 1965

In the cold and dark, identical twin brothers Tony and Augie stood shivering in a nineteen-degree temperature waiting for the owner of a drugstore across the street to close his shop and leave for home.

Tony wore a green military coat and hat with earflaps tied under his chin. Augie wore a long wool coat he had stolen from a restaurant cloakroom. It was too big to be stylish, but it was warm and roomy enough to hide a week's worth of pilfered groceries from the Acme grocery store near his house.

A week after the heist of the coat, Augie had his girlfriend sew on a yellow peace sign on his right shoulder. As the brothers waited, steam from their breaths mixed with smoke from their Marlboros.

"I'm freezing my nuts off. Thought he closed at ten," Tony said.

"He was supposed to."

"It's almost ten thirty, and I'm freezing my nuts off."

"Enough with your nuts already. He's just cleaning up."

Minutes later, the overhead lights went out in the store, and the brothers saw the old man lock the front door and walk away.

"You're sure the back door will be open?" Tony asked.

"I told you a million fucking times, Pauly put a key under the trash can in the back."

After the owner disappeared around the corner, the brothers left the shadows of an alley and jogged across the deserted street, then on to the back of the drugstore, where they found over a dozen trash cans.

"Fuck me," Augie said.

For the next few minutes, the brothers got on their hands and knees in the snow and ice and looked for the key under the trash cans. They found it under can number eight.

Holding the key up like a prize won at a county fair, Tony smiled at Augie, moved to the back door, and unlocked it. The brothers moved inside, where each pulled out clunky flashlights they had stolen from a hardware store a week earlier.

"The cigarettes are up front. I'll go …" Before Tony could finish his sentence, the store lights came on, and the brothers saw three Trenton cops with guns drawn, standing in an aisle filled with various headache and athlete's foot medications.

The largest of the cops had a smile on his face and said, "Hi, gentlemen, guess you didn't know the store closed at ten."

"Shit," the brothers said in stereo.

After two nights in an eight-by-ten jail cell, the brothers, along with their court-appointed attorney, stood before Judge Robert Jackson. Their sobbing mother sat behind them.

"Boys, this is the third time you've been in my courtroom in the last year, and I'm confused. You're both decent students and come from a good family. I know your dad and understand your mom does the best she can without him around anymore, but not having a father at home isn't an excuse for the trouble you boys keep getting into. I don't get it."

The brothers' attorney tried to intercede. "Your Honor, if I may address the court …"

"No, Counselor, you may not address the court. I want to hear directly from these boys before I sentence them both to jail for five years on a parole violation for car theft, stealing from a Schaefer Beer truck, and now breaking into a drugstore."

The boys' mother wailed in the background after she heard the judge's terse comments, while Tony and Augie said nothing and looked down at the floor.

"Boys, I'm not fooling around here. You either tell me what's going on or you're both going to jail, today."

"Judge … " Augie said before being interrupted.

"Address me as Your Honor."

"Yes, sir, Your Honor. First of all, we're really, really sorry for what we've done, but honestly, we think it sounds a lot worse than it really was. See, that car rap thing was just us going on a little joyride around the block for a few minutes. If we hadn't got stopped by those fuzz, I mean police officers, for going just five miles over the limit, we were gonna bring that car back, and no one would've even known we took it."

"That's right, Your Honor, see, we never drove a Cadillac before and wanted to see what it was like, and it was pretty cool. Besides, that fat guy who went into the bar left the keys in the ignition, you know, so he was kinda just askin' us to take that Eldo for a little spin," Tony helpfully pointed out.

"And that beer thing was just kind of a joke, ya know? We'd been playin' baseball in the park over on Third Avenue, and all the guys got hot and thirsty and … " Augie said.

"And we saw that beer truck with the back door open parked in front of Joe's Tavern and didn't think they'd miss a few bottles," Tony added.

"It was seven cases, boys," the judge reminded the beer thieves.

But Tony had an explanation. "Yes, Your Honor, but you know what they say." Augie joined Tony in a brief musical duet: "Schaefer is the one beer to have when you're having more than one."

Tony and Augie laughed at their clever use of a TV beer commercial. The judge did not laugh. Their mother cried. Their attorney shook his head and looked up at the ceiling of the courthouse.

"And the drugstore?" the judge asked wearily.

"Well, Your Honor, you see, that was a little mistake," Augie explained.

"No, I would say that was a big mistake, son," the judge corrected.

"Yes, sir, Your Honor, that was a real big mistake, but in a way, we were just protecting our mom, see."

"What?! How in the world were you two protecting your mother by robbing a drugstore at ten at night? And this better be good."

"Well, Your Honor," Tony said in a voice dripping with self-sacrifice, "see, our mom doesn't know we smoke or need to use rubbers … er … I mean condoms sometimes, you know what I mean, and so …"

The brothers' mother achieved a new level of despair when she heard her boys' confession to smoking and premarital sex as an excuse for the theft of a drugstore … to the judge.

Augie added, "See, Your Honor, we knew it was wrong, but we wanted to stock up on those kinda personal items before we went to Atlantic City this summer and, you know …"

The muffled laughter in the courtroom was in sharp contrast to the crying of the boys' mother and caused the judge to struggle to comprehend what he had just heard. As he stared down at the brothers, he slowly took off his glasses, rubbed his eyes, then addressed the boys in a steady, even voice and tried his utmost to control his disbelief. "Boys, after twenty-five years on this bench … those are clearly and without question the dumbest, most asinine, most ridiculous, BS-laden set of excuses I have ever heard."

Tony tried to explain. "But, Your Honor …"

"Son, this is the time for both of you to just shut up and listen. Because I'm afraid if you keep talking, I'm going to have to give each of you ten years on Rikers." With the judge's words echoing around the walls of the courtroom, the twins' mother reached a new decibel level of wailing.

"Yes, sir, Your Honor," the brothers said in unison.

"Here's the deal, guys, and it's the only deal you're going to get from me. I'm going to let you boys decide your own sentences, because I've decided you two are about as guilty as anyone has ever been in this courtroom. Here it is: you can either go to jail today for five years each, or join the marines … today, or go to college. If it's college, it must be an out-of-state school, and I'll need to see your grades every semester. If either of you drops out or your GPA drops below a C average, I'll get *both* of your butts extradited back here in a heartbeat and put you *both* in jail."

The brothers' mother stopped crying, stood, and addressed the judge. "Your Honor, you have my word, both of them will go to college."

"Well, what will it be, boys, jail, college, or the marines?"

Tony had a question for the judge. "Your Honor, how old do you have to be to enlist in the marines?"

After the hearing, the boys lingered in front of the courthouse and engaged in an animated conversation with their mother and their attorney, who said, "Listen, guys, you just got a huge break in that courtroom, but if you don't get into college for the fall semester, that judge is going to throw your butts in prison."

"They both have the grades, and their daddy and I saved up some money for them to go to college. We'll just have to start applying."

"It won't be easy at this late date. Guys are flooding college admission departments because of this Vietnam thing and the draft, so you better get cracking on the applications right away. There are some new colleges out west you might check out, like Parsons College in Iowa, and John F. Kennedy College, and a brand-new school called Hiram Scott College, both in Nebraska. But like I said, don't wait. I have a feeling the judge will want to see you back in his court in a week or two to see if you have applied anywhere."

While their attorney and mother spoke, the brothers soon lost interest in that conversation and instead looked at the steady stream of braless, miniskirt-clad girls who walked past on the courthouse plaza and smiled at each one. Many of the girls smiled back at the brothers, who looked like variations of Frankie Avalon, the old '50s rock-and-roll singer. Both were good looking, funny, cool, had really white teeth and slicked-back, shiny, wavy black hair.

Tony thought of himself as more of an eventual war hero than a movie star, with the Vietnam War being his path to fame and glory. And eventually, money. A lot of money. He also, despite being an identical twin, felt he was much better looking than his brother.

Augie thought that war was total bullshit and was afraid his Audie Murphy wannabe twin brother would end up in Vietnam and get his fucking head blown off when he tried to be a hero.

Tony had wanted to enlist when the judge gave him that option, but his mother made him promise to go to college for at least a year before he did. That promise was tough on Tony, but he loved his mother and agreed to wait before he enlisted … but only for one year.

Tony did not want to miss the war that was going to be his personal path to international recognition as the greatest killer of commies the world had ever seen. And the handsomest.

Tony's plan was that inevitable international recognition of his war exploits would obviously lead to a career in films, where the world would also marvel that someone who could kill so many commies could also play super-sensitive scenes as Cary Grant did in *An Affair to Remember*, especially that last scene where Grant finds that picture he had painted on Deborah Kerr's wall in her bedroom. That scene always made Tony cry, although no one ever knew that.

Of course, there was also the well-known fact that women, especially superhot Jersey women, were always attracted to great-looking, commie-killing war heroes. That was a particularly well-known fact in Trenton, New Jersey, in 1965.

The biggest disappointment for Augie in the judge's order was that he felt he had what it took to be very a successful criminal, especially in Trenton, where such skills as guts, daring, toughness, and, in some cases, foot speed were highly coveted by the local mafia types, who were always on the lookout for up-and-coming talent.

The only uncertainty Augie had was if, in a pinch or given a direct order from a capo, he could really kill somebody. "I guess I could shoot somebody if they broke in our house and tried to rob us, like steal our TV, or tried to hurt Mom, or our dog, but not so sure I could knock off some dude just because he pissed off somebody," Augie had told Tony.

What confused a lot of folks in the neighborhood about Augie and Tony was they liked to beat the living hell out of each other for no apparent reason. They could be walking down the street on a sunny day just shooting the shit, when one of them would haul off and slug the other in the arm as hard as he could. This would lead the accosted brother to retaliate with a series of punches to the arms and back of his only sibling.

Sometimes these skirmishes would draw crowds, and money would be wagered on who would win the latest battle. Of course, the brothers did have some rules for these altercations, but the most important one was they could only throw body shots, since they agreed they were both too good looking to risk having a punch by one that could forever damage the utter handsomeness of the other.

They also imposed a "no hitting or kicking in the nuts" rule, which could lead to even temporary sexual performance issues, which, of course, could then lead to an unfair reflection on the other brother even if he was operating with two good nuts.

However, there were accidents. On a trip to Atlantic City the previous summer, the brothers were walking on the beach when Tony decided that was as good a time as any to unload on Augie's right arm. That led to some serious retaliation from Augie, including a wayward punch that caught Tony on the jaw, knocking him down.

"Hey, asshole, remember, no headshots!" Tony yelled.

Bending over his brother, Augie said, "Hey, man. I'm really, really sorry. Are you okay? That was an accident. Here, take a free shot, I deserve it."

"Naw, just be careful, man. You could've hurt our face."

As they were about to begin another round of more carefully placed punches, two good-looking girls in bikinis walked by and smiled at the brothers.

"Yo, girls, slow down a little and let's talk. We think we love youse," Tony said. Their fighting was done for the day.

Despite their slugfests, the brothers loved each other. They would also come to the defense of the other if anyone said something negative about one of them or tried to pick a fight. Guys soon learned if you got into a fight with one of them, you would end up fighting both.

A week after applying to several schools in Iowa, Nebraska, and Oklahoma, they learned Scottsbluff would be where they would pursue their higher education. Their mother and Judge Jackson were pleased. The brothers were also pleased … they would not be going to jail. At least for now.

Now, all they had to do was find Scottsbluff on a map.

Chapter 7

New York City: March 1965

Madison Square Garden was packed with fans from Villanova and Seton Hall wishing death and destruction on each other and their respective teams. Seton Hall was the underdog, but they were hanging tough, even though they had no answer for Nova Wildcat Jimmy Clark, a 6'8", 210-pound junior who was *on* that night, and that made him virtually unstoppable. He scored from the outside, the inside, the foul line, and on three occasions on fast break dunks that rocked the rims and brought Wildcat fans to their feet with "Jimmy, Jimmy, Jimmy" chants.

In the stands were a half-dozen NBA scouts who came to see if Jimmy was worthy of all the superlatives they had heard about him. He was. In fact, he was better than they had heard.

A scout from the Knicks said, "The son of a bitch can score. See that rotation on his jump shot? Beautiful."

"He's too small for a big forward, but not sure he's quick enough for a guard," the Celtics scout said.

"I'm not sure he can't play a big guard. Hell, the way he shoots and runs the court, a team will find a spot for him," the Bulls scout observed.

At that moment, Jimmy blocked a shot on a 6'10" center, grabbed the loose ball, streaked down the court, and threw down a vicious two-handed dunk that put away the game.

"Yeah, somebody will find a spot for that bastard. He can play," the Knicks scout said.

"I see him as a late first or early second-round pick," the Bulls scout noted.

"Yep, that young man can make some big money playing this game," the Celtics scout said.

Two hours after the game, Jimmy and his teammates had successfully smuggled a case of beer up the elevator to their floor in a New York hotel. Their train back to Philadelphia was not until eleven thirty the next morning, and they felt they had earned a bit of celebration after they had held off Seton Hall and likely sealed an NCAA bid.

When the players exited the elevator, they saw a group of older women halfway down the hallway. All the guys had to do was ignore the women and enter their room with their beer. In fact, four of the five guys did just that. But Jimmy did something else. He waved at the women, smiled, then turned around, dropped his pants, and mooned the group before he entered his room.

Two days later Jimmy was awakened at 7 a.m. by the team manager knocking on his dorm room door. "Hey, Jimmy, Coach wants to see you." After getting no response from Jimmy, the manager knocked again. "C'mon, Jimmy, Coach wants me to drag your ass to his office."

Finally, a groggy Jimmy cracked his dorm room door, peered out, and said, "Damn, Bobby, it's barely light outside."

"Tell me about it. But he said he needs to see you right away."

"Damn, all right. Give me five minutes."

"Okay, but he told me to wait for you."

After a ten-minute walk from his dorm to his coach's office in twenty-degree weather, Jimmy was finally awake and wondered if, based on his on-court performance the previous weekend against Seton Hall, maybe a pro scout wanted to meet him and contacted his coach to set it up.

The idea of playing in the NBA with and against his boyhood idols had consumed Jimmy for a decade, and he knew he had the talent to make it at the highest level. He also knew he needed to work on some aspects of his game and was willing to do whatever it took to get where he wanted to go.

He had grown up poor in a broken family in North Philly, a rough neighborhood, and never saw his father after first grade. Despite a fatherless home, he had successfully stayed away from local gangs and drugs and instead focused on getting the grades that would get him onto one of the Big Five teams. And, of course, he also focused on basketball.

At nine years old he learned how to calculate percentages so he could track to the fourth decimal point his free throw accuracy. He would shoot three hundred shots a day until he could hit over 80 percent with his eyes shut. His obsessiveness caused inflammation in his right arm due to overuse. So, he began shooting left-handed until his right arm healed, which improved his shooting and ball handling skills with both hands.

Hour after hour, day after day, he would move around the court and shoot a basketball that became worn and smooth until his perfected form almost precluded the possibility of a miss. When he did miss, he would curse himself and shoot until whatever flaw had occurred was erased.

In addition to perfecting his shot, Jimmy worked on his ball handling skills, perfected a crossover, a jab step, and did twenty full-court wind sprints every day to increase his speed and endurance.

When he wasn't on the court, he would be in the library or working with an academic tutor to make sure his grades were up to snuff. It was hard work, but Jimmy's dream now appeared to be within his grasp.

La Salle, St. Joseph, Penn, and Temple had all recruited him as early as ninth grade, but he knew that Villanova and its Main Line campus was where he wanted to go. While only a few miles as the crow flies from where he was raised, it was a whole world away in terms of culture, sophistication, and beauty, and would provide him an opportunity to pay back his mother for what she had sacrificed to help get him a degree from such a prestigious university.

"Hey, Jimmy, great game the other night," a student walking with a small group of fans said.

"Thanks, man," Jimmy replied with a wave and smile.

As the group surrounded Jimmy, congratulating him on another All-American performance, Jimmy smiled and joked, "I heard you guys up in the stands yellin' my name and tellin' me to score and I thought it was the cops, so I figured I best make you all happy." The group laughed and the conversation lasted for several minutes, while Jimmy talked to the group of fans. A smile never left his face.

Beyond his obvious basketball skills, Jimmy was popular on campus for that big smile, along with his obvious native intelligence, wit, and sense of humor.

He also knew he was developing what could be long-term personal relationships that would serve him well after his professional basketball career was over. He intended to come back in the offseasons and get a master's degree and then maybe get into coaching or even be a radio and TV play-by-play announcer when his playing days were over. It was all part of his plan.

Despite other career opportunities that Jimmy had considered, he knew that basketball, at least for the time being, was his identity. It's what separated him from the other guys on campus, even other basketball players. Everyone knew Jimmy was different. It's what made former players look him up when they returned to campus to see a game because they knew someday Jimmy was going to be an NBA star. Most everyone also knew Jimmy had earned what was coming to him. He worked hard in the classroom and on the court, usually being the first to be at practice and the last to leave.

While not a "scholar" in the classroom, Jimmy studied hard and took his classes seriously. In the second semester of his sophomore year, he made the Dean's List and, as a surprise to his mother, had the letter from the school framed and gave it to her as a birthday present. After unwrapping it, she cried for an hour.

After Jimmy had waited outside his coach's office for five minutes, the secretary opened the door, and he saw the coach, athletic director, and school president sitting around a table with papers in front of them.

"Jimmy, come on in and sit down," the coach said.

Jimmy nodded at the men in the office, who seemed to look away from him and back at the papers on the table.

"Hey, Coach," Jimmy said casually, although something made it difficult for him to speak.

"Got a question for you, Jimmy. Was it you who dropped trou in the hallway of the hotel after the game on Saturday night and proceeded to show your ass to a bunch of women?"

"What? No, I mean, it wasn't me … I mean, I don't remember …"

"You mean you wouldn't remember mooning a bunch of ladies on Saturday night in a New York City hotel?"

"Coach, I don't remember …"

"If it wasn't your black ass, then whose black ass was it, Jimmy? The only other two Black guys on the team are five-foot-ten."

"Not sure, Coach …"

The coach looked at the other men around the table and shook his head. "Jimmy, one of those women you mooned was my wife. She's seen you play a hundred times and recognized you, not your ass, but your face. One of the other women is the mother of our Dean of Academic Studies, who is an ordained priest. She recognized you too. Jimmy, you fucked up, son."

"But, Coach …"

"Jimmy, you're through here. Make sure you turn in all your gear before you leave campus. We'll honor your scholarship until the end of this term, but then you're on your own."

"But, Coach, I …"

"Jimmy, you're a hell of a player, and I'm sick about this, but there's nothing any of us can do about this situation. The papers already know about it, and it'll be all over radio and TV later today. We're going to say you have been removed from the team and expelled from school for a rule's infraction. Nothing more."

"Coach, the Knicks and Celtics are scouting me. I could get drafted after next year … but … if I leave school like this …"

"Like I said, Jimmy, our hands are tied over this, but I have an old friend, Forddy Anderson, who coached at Michigan State and is a hell of a coach and a good guy. He's starting a basketball program out in Nebraska somewhere. I'll give him a call and see if he'll give you a chance. That's the best I can do, Jimmy."

For several moments, Jimmy remained seated, stunned by what he had just heard. While his brain tried to process what he realized was the worst possible news he could ever hear—aside from the death of his mother—he was overcome by nausea and a cold sweat, both of which made him dizzy and unable to speak or move.

"Jimmy, you've got to leave now," the coach said.

Jimmy nodded and, after he left the coach's office, wandered around campus for almost two hours, not quite sure that what had just happened really happened. He kept hoping it had been a bad dream and he was still in his dorm room asleep after studying the night before for an American History exam that he would now never take.

As was usually the case, when he passed other students on campus, they smiled and said hi, but this time Jimmy did not or could not respond. All he could think of was that his carefully thought-out and, to that point, well-executed life plan in a matter of just a few minutes had cratered, and he felt a sense of loss that was as profound as it was emotionally dangerous.

As he walked, he talked to himself and voiced his biggest concern, which was not basketball. "Mama, I did something real stupid, and I'm real, real sorry."

When he entered his mother's row home just off Spring Garden Street a few hours later, he was prepared to give her the fictional story he had been rehearsing in his head to soften the blow as much as she could. Instead, she beat him to it when she greeted him with a hug, and said, "James, baby, I heard it on KYW. The whole city is talkin' about it. But what's done is done. No use cryin' about it now. Your coach called and gave me the name of some coach in Nebraska, who said he has a spot for you on his team and will give you a full ride."

"But, Mom, it was *Villanova*."

"Those tight-ass fish-eaters can go straight to hell. Those white ladies see a fine, young black ass like yours for the first time and try to ruin your life. You'll show all of them. They can kick you out of school, but they can't take away that fine jump shot of yours, baby."

Chapter 8

Scottsbluff High School: 1965

From the podium of the high school auditorium, the principal addressed the audience. "Ladies and gentlemen. I am very pleased to announce that this year's Class Valedictorian is Alan Jordan."

The small audience in the auditorium applauded as Alan, dressed in a new blue blazer, gray slacks, and red tie, basked in the attention. "Way to go, Big Al," someone yelled. Another voice among a group of female students said, "We all really, really love you, Alan."

The principal continued, "Alan not only achieved a perfect 4.0 grade point average and a perfect score on his SAT, but he was also an Eagle Scout, captain of the Nebraska State Debate Team, won medals in several rodeo events up in Cheyenne, and placed second in the state in the cross-country meet in Omaha last fall, all while working part time at Scottsbluff General Hospital. You've had one heck of a year, Alan."

While the principal spoke, Alan sat on the stage behind him and made faces and waved to members of the student body, mostly girls, who waved back and threw him air kisses.

When the principal finally welcomed Alan to the podium, the audience broke out in applause once again while Alan ambled slowly across the stage with a smile on his face. He sported short-cropped hair, wore wire-rimmed glasses, and for a skinny young man who was only 5'8", he had a cocky walk, like a mini-John Wayne. Like he knew stuff other people did not know. He did.

After he adjusted the microphone, he stared into the audience for a few moments, then opened his speech by saying, "Thank you, thank you very much," using his famous and spot-on Elvis Presley imitation.

Over the next thirty minutes, Alan regaled the audience with a series of impressions he had refined over the years by watching old movies with his mother.

Each impression from a famous actor dealt with a current issue that was facing the world. While the quotes were in some cases hilarious, others took on a serious note. In all cases, the people listened to a young man everyone knew was destined for something far bigger than Scottsbluff, Nebraska; like being a big-time lawyer, CEO of a Fortune 500 company, or president of the whole damn country.

Near the end of his speech, Alan looked out into the audience, saw his mother, and waved to her. She waved back with tears in her eyes. "Well, Mom, we did it. As I look back, I'm not sure how we did it, but we did. After Dad died, it was all on you, and you came through as you always have. When I go off to Yale next year, I'll be excited about what the future has in store, but whatever happens, it will be because of you, Mom." The audience erupted in cheers.

"Finally, as trouble brews in Southeast Asia, there is a possibility that some in this room may have to go fight in that war, although today it's being called only a *conflict* or *police action* by the press. But American boys my age, like my cousin Paul, in Kansas, have already died over there, so that *conflict* sure sounds a lot like a war to me. It's up to all of us to make sure that war doesn't widen and take more Americans."

The crowd was glued to Alan as he spoke in a tone that was of someone much older. "Remember what Einstein said, 'It is my conviction that killing under the cloak of war is nothing but an act of murder.'"

Alan paused for several moments as Einstein's words sunk in.

"For the sake of all the young men and women who end up fighting the wars our leaders instigate, I hope our country listens to and takes heed of Albert's words. He sounds like a pretty smart guy to me. Well, Scottsbluff, please wish me luck in New Haven next fall when I enter my first year of pre-law, but remember, I'll never forget Scottsbluff!"

While most of the audience cheered and applauded Alan as he departed the stage, many older men sat in stony silence, not appreciating that Alan "got political" during his speech. Besides, they thought what many others thought—it's better to fight the commies over there than in our own backyard.

A week after his graduation ceremony, Alan's mother called him in from outside, where he had been reading Yale's Orientation Booklet on the back porch.

"Hey, Mom, what's up?"

"Honey, my doctor just called and said I have a little problem."

Knowing his mother's penchant for understatement, Alan sat down next to her and took her hand. "You talking about that numbness in your hands and feet?"

"Yes, and some other things."

"What did he say?"

"I'm going to get other opinions because you know how these doctors mess everything up and …"

"What did he say, Mom?" As he asked the question, Alan's voice lowered to a whisper, and in his gut he feared her answer.

"Well, he said I had something called ALS and …"

"Amyotrophic lateral sclerosis, Lou Gehrig's disease."

"Yes, that's what he called it, but like I said, what does he know?"

For several moments something rare occurred. Alan was speechless. He rose from his chair and paced around the living room as a million thoughts went through his brain.

"Alan, he could be wrong. No use worrying about this now. We'll just go on with everything, and in a year or two, they might find a cure."

"Sure, Mom."

When his mother had begun to exhibit a long list of symptoms months earlier, Alan had gone to the library and read up on possible causes. He also spoke to several doctors in town under the pretense he was considering medical school and had narrowed down several explanations of her symptoms. ALS was one of them.

He knew there was no cure and did not doubt his mom's doctor's diagnosis. But he knew within seconds of hearing what his mother had said that his plans had changed.

"Okay, Mom, I've decided I'm going to call Yale today and put off enrolling until next year. You know, you're probably right and your doctor is likely wrong, but I'll just stay here for a year, and when you're better next year ..."

"But, Alan, you can't miss out on Yale, and you might get drafted if you don't go to college next fall."

"I'll go to that new college here in town. I think their draft-preventing capabilities are as good as Yale's, and I'll go to New Haven next year. No big deal. By the way, let's go out for pizza tonight."

Alan knelt down next to his mother's chair, and they held each other for several minutes while both sobbed.

CHAPTER 9

SAN DIEGO: FALL 1965

JT — As usual, the weather was perfect in San Diego for my long-awaited drive to the wilds of Nebraska. My dad's atlas said it was over twelve hundred miles away, which made it about one thousand miles farther than I had ever been from home.

While the reasons I was heading to Nebraska were painful, embarrassing, and out-and-out stupid, the idea of what I saw as a one-year adventure had me looking forward to getting out of San Diego and away from all the questions people were asking me and my parents about why I was not headed to Annapolis.

I had spent the last week packing what I might need and bought some stuff I had never owned before, like a heavy winter coat. I was curious about snow and wondered if I would be able to drive in the white stuff.

After I checked the tire pressure and oil for the third time in the last week, I was about to close the hood of the Ford when I heard a voice from behind me.

"Hey, where you goin'?"

Jon turned and saw who he remembered as the little girl named Anna who lived across the street. She was no longer little.

"Nebraska."

"Why?"

"The beaches."

"Don't see your surfboard."

"Sold it and a bunch of other stuff. Actually, I'm going to college there."

"Thought you were going to Annapolis."

"I was."

Anna crossed the street and leaned up against Jon's Ford. She was a year younger than Jon and had short dark hair and dark eyes that gave her a Natalie Wood kind of look that Jon had somehow overlooked before. She was cute, trim, clearly smart, and just a little cocky.

"By the way, I'm Anna, and to be honest, which I am wont to be, I heard what happened with you and Valerie."

Jon looked up from washing his windows. "Guess everybody did. By the way, I'm Jon."

"I know who you are," Anna said. She began to walk around the Ford as if appraising it.

"Really?"

"Sure, all the girls in my class know who you are. Watched you play basketball and tennis."

Jon stopped cleaning his windows, leaned back against the Ford, and realized Anna was worth his undivided attention.

"That wasn't fair, you know, what Valerie did."

"Fair or not, I'm going to Nebraska."

"My sister told me Valerie said she was going to marry you two years ago. She guaranteed it to the other girls."

"Well, she didn't."

"My sister also said she knew she wasn't pregnant after two months but didn't tell you, so you'd marry her."

Jon stared at Anna for several moments. "Your sister told you that?"

"Yes, and I believe it. Valerie is the type of girl who would do such a thing."

Jon turned and went back to washing his car windows. "Guess the joke's on her, then."

"Bad joke. I mean what happened to you—getting kicked off the teams, losing your appointment to the Naval Academy, all that—was terrible."

"Too late to worry about that stuff now. By the way, weren't you just a little kid like a week ago?"

"I'm seventeen."

"Really? You're a junior?"

"Yes, going to Stanford next year. Early acceptance and a full academic ride."

"Good for you. Damn, seventeen. And Stanford," Jon said as he noticed Anna really was a Natalie Wood lookalike. Only cuter and probably smarter.

"Too bad we never really talked before. I noticed you lots of times. I mean I'd seen you across the street and at school all these years and …"

"Guess I thought you were just a little kid and …"

"And you were too busy doing Valerie."

Jon hesitated, forced a smile, then said, "Yeah, well, that was obviously a poor life decision."

"Yeah, I guess it was."

For several moments, Anna and Jon stared at each other, hoping the other might say something.

"Yeah, guess so. Well, I need to hit the road. Nebraska's cornfields await," Jon said as he entered the Ford.

"I think the money crop out there is beets." Anna moved close to Jon's open window, inches from his face.

Jon looked up at Anna and smiled. "Good luck this year at school."

"Thanks. You know, if you get lonely in Nebraska, you could always write me, and I'll write back, you know, like San Diego pen pals."

"Yeah, that would be great. I'd like that."

"Me too. Well, drive carefully, and don't forget to write," Anna said as she lingered near Jon's face for several moments.

"I will. I sure know your address. Tell your folks I said goodbye."

Anna smiled and walked back to her side of the street. Jon backed out of his driveway and smiled at Anna. But before he could drive away, Anna moved quickly to the driver's side of the car again. "Wait!" she yelled.

Jon stopped the car. Anna bent down, put her arms around his neck, and kissed him. The kiss lasted for nearly a minute.

Finally, they broke free, and Jon looked up at Anna. "How old did you say you were?"

"Seventeen, but I've wanted to do that since I was twelve. Remember what I said, drive carefully, and don't forget to write," Anna ordered before she walked away.

When she got to the other side of the street, Jon said, "Hey, Anna, I definitely won't forget to write."

Anna waved, smiled, and went into her parents' mid-century, trilevel house. For several moments Jon stared at her front door before he smiled too and drove away.

> JT — When I watched Anna go back to her house, I couldn't help but think that all through that miserable time with Valerie, I had this cute, smart little brunette living just across the street from me who had wanted to kiss me for five years. It confirmed once and for all I was an idiot, although my dad never had any doubts.
>
> After Valerie told me of my pending fatherhood, word got out, and things began to go to shit. Within two weeks I was informed by the Naval Academy they would seek admirals elsewhere, presumably from a group of virginal young road men, and I was on my way to Nebraska, which I had to find on a map since all I knew of that state before was it was north of the equator and south of the Arctic Circle.
>
> While I had gotten A's in US geography and, of course, had heard of Nebraska, mostly because of their football team, all those states like Iowa, Kansas, Wyoming, Montana, and Nebraska just sort of blended together and were "out there" somewhere. They were places I never had any desire to visit, but here I was going to a place where I would spend an entire year of my life.

After what had happened with the academy, my grades going to crap, getting kicked off the teams, and the embarrassment of it all, Valerie called me and almost casually told me she wasn't pregnant after all. And now, like magic, we had nothing to worry about. She also told me that we were formally breaking up, and that she was now dating a guy from Balboa who was headed for West Point. I guess she liked guys in uniforms.

For several moments after her call, I toyed with the idea of strangling Valerie and going to San Quentin for the rest of my life rather than Nebraska, but I decided instead to just leave town for a while and see what happened. After all, I was learning plans seldom worked out as planned, so what's the fucking point?

After finding Nebraska on a map, I went to AAA, tracked my route to the northeast with a bright yellow highlighter, put it on my dashboard, and hit the road toward the great American Middle West, which I never could separate in my head from the Midwest. I assumed there was a difference but at that point didn't care.

After two days of driving into the most desolate terrain I had ever seen and an overnight stopover in a small town in Utah, I came to a sign that confirmed my destination actually existed. It said, "Scottsbluff 91 miles."

I turned right and, after forty-five minutes, began to see my first bluff in the distance. In fact, it was Scott's Bluff, which I later read had been named after an unfortunate young trapper named Hiram Scott, who was only twenty-three years old when he got lost on his way to Missouri, froze to death, and yet had a bluff named after him.

By the way, I think a bluff is a really big hill, a small mountain, or a messed-up mesa, not sure. Also not sure how getting frozen to death on a bluff warrants having that same bluff named after you when all you seemingly did was freeze to death, which in my mind would not be all that difficult a task for anyone if they set their mind to it. But apparently, Nebraskans back in the day didn't grade all that tough.

As I drove, I wondered: If I ran off the road and was killed in my Ford, would they name the road I was on "Jon's Road"? Those are the things you think about after two days alone in a Ford.

At long last and with a desire for a hot meal and to stop being in what felt like perpetual motion, I came to a large, slightly tilted wooden sign bordered by yellow and purple flowers I did not recall seeing in California. It said: "Welcome to Scottsbluff."

CHAPTER 10

SCOTTSBLUFF: 1965

In anticipation of the first day of classes the following week, the city of Scottsbluff was bustling with new students and professors arriving, along with some area residents who came into town to see what young people from Chicago, New York, Philadelphia, LA, Washington, DC, and other big city outposts actually looked like.

The city council stood together on a street corner near the Lincoln Hotel, which had been converted to a dormitory for men, and smiled at the realization of the mayor's well-planned, albeit stolen, vision to save the town from financial ruin. Betty was not among them.

"Never thought it would happen this quick," Harold said.

"Vic's Pizza and the Eagle Café are packed. Both got waiting lines," Buck noted.

"Same with the motels. All sold out for two weeks," Earl reported.

Irwin added, "Charlie down at the Esso Station ran out of gas. Second time this week. Mayor, you sure hit the jackpot with this idea. Maybe we'll name a bluff after you."

"Well, sometimes you just get an idea out of nowhere, and you have to go with it," the mayor said in a humble tone, downplaying his utter brilliance.

> JT — That first day in town was kind of a madhouse. Not sure what I was expecting, but it wasn't what I saw. I don't think that any of the locals, who we ended up calling "Townies," had ever seen that many cars in town at the same time. Especially *those* cars. There were

Corvettes, Mercedes, Porsches, Cadillac Rivieras, and Thunderbirds with Jersey, New York, Illinois, and Pennsylvania license plates. They were all cruising up and down Broadway with guys hanging out the windows, trying their best to convince young Scottsbluff girls to risk their virtue by climbing inside one of their exotic cars. To the delight and surprise of some guys, many girls did.

After circling the block several times, Jon pulled up in front of the Lincoln Hotel, which was to be his home, along with a couple of hundred other students for the 1965–66 school year.

The hotel had opened on December 31, 1918, and had served as the only local hotel for decades, although it was seldom filled and went years without turning a significant profit.

When the college was looking for rooms for students, they cut a deal with the hotel's owners, which included a five-year lease to ensure 100 percent capacity in return for a reduced room rate. It was the kind of deal that worked for everyone.

Jon exited his Ford and entered the Lincoln Hotel, carrying two leather suitcases and a duffle bag filled with two pairs of blue jeans, underwear, and socks. Across the street from the Lincoln, a group of a dozen WWII veterans carried signs of their unbridled support of the Vietnam War, just to let the new student population know where Scottbluffians stood on the subject.

On the other side of the street, three dozen students yelled anti-war chants. On that day, the students prevailed mainly because they had better and more creative signs that used swear words in ways not seen before by Scottsbluff citizens.

When he entered the hotel/dorm, Jon saw sixty to seventy students lounging around the lobby. Some were on chairs, others on wide bay windows that overlooked the street, and still others on the floor. Some read books, some talked, some made out. In fact, many made out.

The background music that blasted through the lobby speakers during this activity ranged from the Beach Boys to the Rolling Stones to Joni Mitchell to Marvin Gaye to a local band called the Dynamics, which featured future Eagles bass player and singer Randy Meisner.

Jon wore a denim jacket and jeans. He got approving looks from several girls lounging in the lobby. They seemed to like his semi-long brown wavy hair, as they took note when he ran his fingers through it. One of the girls even mentioned his blue eyes. "He looks a little like Jack Kennedy," a well-proportioned blonde pointed out to her friend.

Jon weaved his way through the lobby to the front desk, where a girl, Vicki, was checking in students, although she appeared to be a bit overwhelmed by all the questions being asked of her. After waiting patiently for several moments, Jon finally got Vicki's attention. "Excuse me, I enrolled a couple weeks ago and was told to come here and get my room assignment."

"What's your name?"

"Jon Taylor, from San Diego, California."

Vicki looked through what looked like over two hundred supposedly alphabetized index cards in a green metal box. When she could not find his card the first time through, she started again, and Jon got worried.

"Ah, here it is," she finally said. "You're in room number three-thirty-eight. Your roommates are Augie and Tony Marinelli. They're brothers from New Jersey."

Vicki handed Jon two keys and pointed to the elevator. "You get two keys, but if you lose them, it's five dollars for a third key."

"Thanks."

After lugging his suitcases and bag onto the elevator, he finally made it to the outside of room 338. From inside, he could hear thuds. Like something was being dropped on the floor. That would have been Augie.

As he was about to put his key in the lock of the door, it flew open, and a nearly naked young man was tossed out the door into the hallway and landed at Jon's feet. That would have been Tony, who looked up and asked, "You the third guy?"

"Yeah, I guess I am."

"Well, either you are, or you aren't."

"Yeah, I'm the third guy. You need some help?"

"Nah, just taking a break. Augie in there is my brother, and he's strong as an ox, even though he looks skinny. Mom says we're identical twins, but I think he looks like shit sometimes. What do you think—who's better looking?"

"I haven't seen him yet. By the way, I'm Jon from San Diego."

"Hiya, I'm Tony, from the greatest fucking state in the whole fucking country, New Jersey. Well, I gotta go back in there and kick Augie's ass, or he'll think I gave up. Come on in and grab your bed."

Jon followed Tony into the room, which featured a 1940 motif including printed wallpaper, faded green carpet, nondescript brown wood furniture, and a black-and-white TV set. Jon waved at Augie, who waved back before he grabbed Tony and flipped him on the floor, then pounded him on the back with a flurry of quick punches. Tony and Augie were shirtless, and Jon could see bright red welts on each of the brothers' bodies. Finally, Augie got Tony in a choke hold, and Tony's face got red and then started to turn blue.

"Give up, you little fucker," Augie strongly suggested.

"Fuck you, asshole," Tony managed to gasp while his loving brother attempted to strangle him.

"I said give up, you little shithead!"

"You gotta kill me first, dickwad," Tony declared as he prepared to suffocate.

"I would, but Mom would be pissed."

"Okay, I'll give up for Mom," Tony struggled to say with what sounded like his last breath.

"Okay, dirtbag, I won't kill you," Augie said as both brothers collapsed onto the floor.

Jon had taken a seat on his bed in the corner of the room while he took in the wrestling match. "Are you guys really brothers?" he asked incredulously.

"Yeah, I'm Augie and he's Tony. We're twins, but I'm the good-looking one. We're from that shithole New Jersey."

"Hi, I'm Jon, from California."

"Why do you hate Jersey?" Tony asked his brother.

"I told you a million times, fuckhead, it's crowded, cold, dirty, and smells like shit, at least most of it."

"You're fucked in the head, Jersey's the greatest; you got the shore, great food, Sinatra's from there—how could you not like Jersey, you asshole?"

The brothers then stood up, apparently ready to fight again, when Jon intervened. "Hey, guys, do we have a bathroom in here? I just got off the road, and I'd like to take a shower."

While Tony put Augie in a headlock, he pointed to the bathroom with his other arm. "Through that door. After you're done, let's all go get a pizza. Not like Jersey pizza, which is the best pizza on the fucking planet, but not bad."

> JT — As I was showering, I could hear a series of thuds and grunts as the brothers from Jersey beat the living crap out of each other. In a bizarre sort of way, the brothers were actually rather entertaining, although the chances of one of them ending up in intensive care seemed pretty high to me.
>
> While they were identical looking in their faces, I could tell them apart by the way each wore their hair. Similar, but enough of a styling difference that I could tell one from the other. Despite their desire to maim each other, you could tell there was an affection there and even some native intelligence that belied a first impression.

After a fifteen-minute wait, Tony, Augie, and Jon sat in a booth in Vic's Pizza across the street from the Lincoln Hotel. In the background Country Joe and the Fish belted out "Feels Like I'm Fixin' To Die" on the jukebox as kids from the East Coast ate surprisingly good Nebraska pizza.

Pizza critic Tony observed, "Jersey pizza is thicker and got more cheese, but this ain't bad."

"You from LA?" Augie asked Jon.

"San Diego, about seventy miles south of LA. How did you guys end up out here?"

"This or jail or the marines. I would've joined the marines but promised Mom I wouldn't enlist until next year," Tony said.

"You guys looked around town yet?"

"Not much to see," Augie said.

"Me and Augie went out to where they're building the new dorm. It's in the middle of a damn cornfield. Guess it won't be done till next year."

As the guys talked, students kept coming in and out of Vic's. In the corner near the front door, a family of four sat and stared at what they perceived as aliens from another planet, not used to seeing that much long hair in one place.

Halfway through their attack on a pepperoni, mushroom, and sausage pizza, a cute blonde walked by the guys' table and smiled at Jon. Tony noticed.

"Hey, Jonny boy, I think that babe likes your look. She's not a Jersey girl, who are the hottest girls on the fucking planet, but she's got a nice rack."

Jon looked up and saw an attractive young woman wearing tight white denim jeans and a blue, cotton, midriff shirt along with a wide smile directed toward Jon.

"She's all yours," Jon said.

"What do you mean? You're not a fag, are you?"

"No, Tony, I'm not a fag. I just had a girl problem last year, that's all, and not looking for more trouble."

Moving on, Augie asked, "What classes you takin'?"

"English, Bio, Western Civ, Speech, and Greek History," Jon said.

"Looks like we're all in the same classes. Guess they aren't offering a lot of options this first year."

As the boys talked, four very tall basketball players walked into Vic's, led by Jimmy from Philadelphia. Each wore a letter jacket from another college including Villanova, Michigan State, Dayton, and Indiana. Their appearance captured the attention of the entire restaurant including Jon and the brothers.

"Holy shit, look at the size of those guys. Guess good old Hiram Scott will have a basketball team," Tony said.

Augie added, "I read the coach, a guy named Forddy Anderson, came here from Michigan State after he got fired there and has recruited a bunch of studs. That Black guy who just walked in here is Jimmy Davis. He played at Villanova until he got kicked out for some bullshit and was All-Big Five."

"That should be fun to watch. But not like Bill Bradley from back at Princeton; that's in New Jersey," Tony volunteered.

"Yeah, I've heard of Princeton and Bill Bradley, but Jimmy Davis there scored thirty-nine points when Villanova beat Princeton last year back in Philly," Jon said.

"No shit?" Augie said.

"No shit. And he held Bradley to twenty-seven points," Jon added for emphasis.

Over the next half hour, a dozen girls walked into Vic's and past the guys' table. Each received the same sophisticated reaction from the brothers: "Yo, honey" or "Yo, baby" were the brothers' consistent lines to woo the opposite sex. It did not seem to work all that well.

JT — The rest of that day I got to know Tony and Augie. They were fun guys and smarter than they let on. I learned they had done reasonably well in school but had been kicked out several times for fighting, not just each other but anyone who liked to fight, which sounded like most of New Jersey.

The brothers also spoke almost reverently about their mother and how she had worked two jobs to keep them in cool clothes and hair spray after their father had left them. It was also clear that Tony saw the Vietnam War as part of his career path, leading to fame, money, and sex with Hollywood starlets, while Augie saw the war as unmitigated bullshit that was going to kill a lot of guys.

Of the two brothers, Augie seemed to be the more thoughtful in terms of researching things like the Vietnam War. For instance, he compared it to the Korean Conflict and drew similarities based on books and articles he had read and would frequently quote. In short, it seemed Augie was more cerebral, and Tony was the more emotional one, not just about the war but about most things.

Yet at the surface level, maybe because they looked so much alike, it was easy for people who first met them to see the same person. They weren't. While they were very much alike in certain ways, below the surface, they were two distinct and separate personalities.

Augie, Tony, and Jon walked through downtown Scottsbluff for the rest of the afternoon. They looked in shop windows since most of the businesses were closed, but the bakery was open, and they bought a half-dozen glazed donuts, which they consumed within five minutes.

When they walked past a group of girls, Tony and Augie did their sophisticated wooing, while Jon stood back and watched the brothers perform their well-rehearsed act.

All three guys were, within a few minutes, able to discern girls from the big cities back East from the local girls, who were still wearing clothes from 1955, including white bobby socks worn with black-and-white saddle shoes.

The local girls also giggled, smiled, and acted embarrassed yet intrigued by the brothers' catcalls and over-the-top comments. On the other hand, the girls from New York, Philly, and even New Jersey had heard it all before and thought the brothers were kind of a pain in the ass, which only encouraged Augie and Tony.

When a car drove by with New Jersey plates, the brothers would repeatedly yell, "Yo, Jersey … fuck yeah," which sometimes elicited the beeping of a horn, further animating the brothers.

Near the Midwest movie theater, a group of war protestors carried more anti-war signs and chanted, "Stop killing babies in Vietnam."

Across the street a group of local young men yelled back, "Stop the commies over there." At one point, someone from the anti-war group was hit in the head with a half-filled beer can, which escalated the rhetoric from both sides of the street. A physical confrontation was averted when a 1954 police cruiser drove by, causing both sides to quickly disperse.

JT — After the sugar rush from the donuts, we walked through a beautiful park at the edge of town. Near a gazebo and a small pond filled with lily pads and ducks, I saw a white tent with a red cross on the side. In front of the tent, a sign read, "Fight Breast Cancer—Exams $10. Be safe or be sorry."

I noticed a line of over twenty women waiting for exams. Outside the tent, I noticed a guy from when I was checking into the Lincoln Hotel earlier in the day who had introduced himself as Ron, from Chicago. I remember thinking at the time it was kind of odd that he was wearing a white medical jacket with a stethoscope hanging down around his neck. I mean, he didn't look like any doctor I had ever met. He was also wearing thick, black, horn-rimmed glasses that appeared at least two sizes too large for what was a rather small skull. He also wore dirty Converse basketball shoes and baggy jeans under his white jacket.

At the park, Ron from Chicago was all business and kept looking down at his chart as if it contained cures for most diseases known to college students.

"Hi, girls, it'll just be a few more minutes," Dr. Ron from Chicago said.

One of the girls in line, a tall blonde, had a question. "Are there nurses inside, I mean, a female nurse?"

Dr. Ron appeared just a bit peeved by the question. "No, just guys, but we're all in premed, so it's okay," Dr. Ron patiently explained.

The tall blonde was persistent. "There's a premed program at this school?"

"Sure, but it's an all-guy program."

As Ron spoke, a guy from Detroit, Chuck, exited the tent wearing a Rolling Stones T-shirt, and said, "Okay, Ronnie, I mean Dr. Smith, it's your turn."

"Hey, Chuck, I was just telling the girls here about the great Hiram Scott College premed program."

"Wha …? Oh yeah, *that* premed program. Oh yeah, being a ladies' breast doctor is going to be cool."

From a distance, Augie, Tony, and Jon watched Chuck and Ron perform.

"A few guys from Chicago and Detroit set up that tent a couple days ago and have felt about a million tits so far," Augie explained with deep admiration in his voice.

"Yeah, and they're making some big-time cash. What a great fucking idea. Wish we would have thought of that," Tony said with reverence for the creativity and entrepreneurial spirit of the guys from Chicago and Detroit.

The tall blonde had her doubts about the exam. "Is there a doctor overseeing all this?"

"Sure, but he's on his lunch break," Chuck explained.

"What is the doctor's name?"

"Dr. Johnson. Look, come on in the tent, and we can save you from cancer," Ron said as he grabbed the blonde by her arm.

"Let go of me, you fucking creep."

> JT — Dr. Ron made the mistake of reaching out to grab the tall blonde's arm again, but she stepped back, leaped into the air, and performed what looked like a ballet step and kicked Chuck in the balls. It was actually a pretty cool athletic move that Augie, Tony, and I rated an eight on a scale of ten.
>
> Poor old Ron sank to his knees, his eyes bulged, and it sounded like he was going to puke. While he was writhing on the ground, the tall blonde and several of her friends walked away. We later learned that Ron, Chuck, and the rest of the doctors were the first students to be expelled from Hiram Scott, which was quite a feat since the school had not even officially opened. We concluded the guys had set a record that could never be broken.
>
> Still, despite some obvious flaws in the execution of their plan, which included that expulsion thing, all of us thought their idea had merit and was worthy of our admiration and respect.
>
> We even respected the blonde who had kicked Ron in the balls when she caught on to the ruse. We also wondered how soon it would be

before Ron and his gang would be drafted and sent to Nam to be wounded or killed. Despite those considerable negatives, we thought their plan, and the results, had certainly been worth the risk.

We later learned the tall blonde was from New York and would end up a dancer for the Rockettes at Radio City Music Hall, which explained the high kick and Ron's pain. "That was a hell of a kick," Augie had accurately noted.

When Tony, Augie, and Jon continued their tour of downtown Scottsbluff, they saw a woman in her late thirties with her hair in a brown hair net. She had a warning for her teenage daughter to stay away from the 1957 T-Bird convertible, which carried two handsome surfer-type guys who sported long blond hair.

"You stay away from those boys, Martha. They are no good and will just be trouble and …"

The T-Bird pulled up next to the curb, and the driver, Jason, had a question. "Wow, are you two sisters?"

The Scottsbluff mother began to protest, but then smiled sheepishly and said, "Oh, my Lord, no, this is my daughter, not my sister, although people do say …"

"Mother? You gotta be kidding me. You look like a high school girl, right, Jason?" Tom, the passenger in the T-Bird from Philadelphia, asked his friend.

"She sure does. I think she's putting us on," Jason said with a wide Hollywood-inspired smile.

"No, really, this is my daughter and …"

As the T-Bird occupants spoke to the mother and daughter, a very large man in bib overalls, who carried a fifty-pound bag of grain over his shoulder, approached. "C'mon, Mary, we need to get back home."

"C'mon, Lurch, we're just talking to your daughters here. We won't do them much harm," Jason said.

"You boys better get … now," Lurch suggested.

The husband grabbed the arms of his wife and daughter and tried to walk around the T-Bird, which moved forward, blocking the husband's path.

"C'mon, Lurch, let us take those girls for a ride."

The husband glared at the surfers, then reached up and pulled a string on the bag of grain and proceeded to empty the entire fifty-pound contents into the convertible, covering the surfers with grain.

A small crowd on the street including Tony, Augie, and Jon laughed as the surfer boys tried to uncover themselves while the family walked away. Although the teenage girl did wave goodbye.

That night Augie and Tony were asleep in their room while Jon stared up at the ceiling.

JT — Despite what I would have to call a pretty good first day in Scottsbluff, I seriously thought about killing myself that night. I know that sounds melodramatic, but I really did think about it, although I wasn't quite sure how I would do it. But it seemed that everything I had worked for all my life had been thrown away because I had been stupid.

I liked Tony and Augie well enough, but I was supposed to have been at Annapolis that first night of college. But here I was in Nebraska, about as far away from an ocean as a person could get. I was homesick too. I even thought of Valerie for a few moments, but to be honest, that had nothing to do with homesickness.

I also felt trapped and forced to be in a place I would never have otherwise chosen. I realized that if it had not been for the likelihood I would have been drafted and sent to fight in a war that I thought was horseshit, I could have sat out college for a year.

Or I could have gotten a temporary job or maybe even worked my way through Europe and stayed in hostels and made some memories while I applied to an Ivy League school where knocking up your girlfriend, who in reality wasn't even knocked up, was not considered a reason to deny admission to someone who had scored a 1378 on his SATs. Aside from some badly needed self-pity, the only good thought that first night in Scottsbluff was of that girl across the street … Anna.

Jon finally closed his eyes at 2 a.m.

CHAPTER 11

ENTREPRENEURISM IS GOOD: OCTOBER 1965

The very first class, on the very first day of classes at Hiram Scott College, was Western Civilization. It began at 8:15 a.m. and took place in a building that had been an old furniture store. Over 150 chair-desk combinations, which appeared to be at least fifty years old, were crammed into a room that had at one time displayed couches, lamps, and bedroom sets.

There was an air of anticipation in the room as the students, most of whom had attended other colleges, waited for the professor to arrive. For at least that first class, no one, it seemed, wanted to be late, although that commitment to punctuality would soon fade.

At precisely 8:15 a.m., the professor, a woman in her mid-twenties who had earned her PhD at Northwestern, took the dais. She appeared nervous, given this was her first college class, and she appeared younger than the mostly male students who sat in front of her.

Augie, Tony, and Jon sat in the same row. Jon sat next to a guy named Alan from Scottsbluff, who, in turn, sat next to a tall Black guy named Jimmy, who Jon recognized from Vic's Pizza the day before.

> JT — That first day of class was kind of surreal. It was the first time I had seen so many Hiram Scott students in one spot. The weird thing was most of them did not look like college students at all. At least what I thought college students looked like. First of all, the vast majority of the students in class that day were guys, and most of them looked at least five years older than the rest of us.

What few women were there also looked older and more sophisticated and well-dressed than what I expected college coeds to be. These women were more intimidating than the men.

I probably wasn't, but I felt I was the youngest person in the room. Even Tony and Augie seemed older than I was, even though I knew they weren't.

The guy who had sat next to me introduced himself as "Alan from Scottsbluff." He was a short, skinny guy with horn-rimmed glasses who wore a pocket protector like the guys back in high school who ended up being doctors or mechanical engineers. He also carried a briefcase, which seemed weird.

The guy next to him was the tall Black guy named Jimmy we had seen the day before getting a pizza. I noticed that during that first class, Jimmy slept through most of it, and Alan took down just about every word the professor said. In fact, he took it down twice, which made no sense to me at all.

Since I had taken several Advanced History classes in high school, I already knew most of what the professor was lecturing on. I noticed that Augie and Tony took a few notes but mostly looked around the room and tried to make eye contact with the few women who were around us. The women did not look back.

After the first class, Tony, Augie, and Jon saw Jimmy get copies of the class notes from Alan and then hand him some cash.

"Thanks, Jimmy. Don't forget we have Biology this afternoon at two."

"I'll be there. What did we learn in Western Civ today? Guess I fell asleep."

"Read your notes. It's all in there," Alan said.

"Okay, see you at two."

Jimmy walked away and Alan headed in the opposite direction but was soon joined by Tony, Augie, and Jon.

"Hey, man, looks like you got a nice little business goin'," Tony said.

"Beats part time at Burger Heaven," Alan said with a grin.

"You some kind of tutor or something?" Augie asked.

"Something like that. I got a call from the assistant basketball coach, who said some of the guys on the team needed some help. So, I threw out a crazy number, and he said yes."

"Sounds cool. By the way, I'm Tony. This is my brother, Augie, and our roommate, Jon."

"Hi, guys, how's it going?"

The four guys walked down the street and looked in store windows at JCPenney, Western Auto, and a cowboy boot store. They also checked out the girls who walked by. They entered the bakery the guys had stopped in the day before and walked out with a bag of donuts, which they ate as they continued their walk.

At a street corner, a young man in an army uniform stepped out from a recruiting office and handed recruiting brochures to the guys. "Hey, fellas, when you're through with all this college crap, maybe you should come protect your country. You can get good pay, cool uniforms that chicks dig, and benefits at the same time. I'm Mick, by the way." He stuck out his hand, but none of them shook it except Tony.

In fact, Tony was very interested in what Mick was saying and carefully read the brochure he had been given. "Have you seen any action, man?" he asked.

"No, not yet, but I sure as hell will. Broke my arm right during basic training, but as soon as I'm all healed, I'm there killin' me some commies."

"Fuck yeah, I can dig that shit," Tony said.

Augie moved next to Tony and said, "C'mon, Tony, let's go get some lunch."

Tony ignored Augie and turned back to Mick with a question. "Hey, man, what's the most commies anyone has ever killed, you know, like a world record?"

"I heard one guy from Atlanta killed over fifty in one fucking day," Mick said, with deep admiration in his voice.

"No shit! How? Machine gun? Grenades? Bayonets?"

"All three."

"Holy fucking wow," Tony said, his admiration at an even higher level.

"Yeah, I can't wait. But you know, you can sign up now and be killin' commies in a couple months."

Augie grabbed Tony by the arm and said, "Come on, brother, let's go eat."

"Yeah but …"

"No buts. You know what you promised Mom."

"Hey, pal, let this man make his own decisions."

Augie turned and got up in Mick's face. "Go fuck yourself, soldier boy. This is family business."

Mick gave Augie a half smile. "If I didn't have this United States Army uniform on, I'd …"

"Yeah, and you'd get your ass kicked from here to Denver, you baby-killing, pussy, motherfucker," Augie hissed.

Tony stepped in between the two and said, "Hey, man, the war sounds cool, but my brother, Augie, here will seriously kick your ass. I mean no shit; he'll wipe you all over this sidewalk, so I wouldn't fuck with him."

Mick and Augie glared at each other for several moments until Mick finally turned away and began handing out brochures to other guys walking down the street.

> JT — I saw that recruiting guy Mick a dozen times over the next few weeks handing out his brochures and telling guys how cool the army was and trying to get them to enlist. Some did. I remember a going away party for a guy from Ohio in the dorm who had decided college life was not for him. He was a tall, wiry guy with blond hair. Nice guy. Don't remember his name. It was a pretty good party if I recall; at least the wiry blond guy got blitzed on his ass.
>
> We later learned that the wiry guy from Ohio was shot in the head by a sniper a couple of months later on his first patrol near the

Cambodian border. After finding out he had been killed, and that Mick had recruited him, rumor had it that Augie had confronted Mick in an alley a week later, kicked the shit out of him, and told him if he ever saw him talking to his brother, Tony, he would kill him. A week later, Mick was transferred to Denver to recruit down there.

Jon watched Alan as he talked to Tony and Augie on the front steps of the Lincoln Hotel.

JT — It seemed incongruous given their disparate backgrounds, but Alan got along very well with Tony and Augie. I think it was because the brothers respected Alan's brains, and he respected their ballsy personalities. In fact, all of us were getting along well, not based on our similarities but rather on our differences.

While the brothers were an "acquired taste," around the dorm and classrooms, everyone seemed to like Alan. Maybe it was because he was no threat to anyone, he was funny as hell, obviously whip-smart, and seemed, for reasons not understood by the rest of us, to attract girls, even the older ones.

A house filled with Hiram Scott students and over a dozen local Scottsbluff girls rocked to a Temptations album enhanced by two kegs of beer.

Tony and Augie watched Alan talk to two semi-hot girls. When the redhead whispered in Alan's ear, he took the opportunity to rub his hand up her thigh. Then moved his other hand up to her side to catch a bit of side boob.

"Look at that. If I did that to a Jersey girl, she'd smack me upside the head," Tony said.

"Hate to tell you this, stud, but that girl is from Jersey," Augie sadly reported.

"No shit. Jersey?"

"No shit. Pennsauken."

"I can't believe a guy who looks like that kid on *Leave It to Beaver* has women hanging on him all the time. Saw him at Vic's the other night with three good-lookin' girls all laughing their asses off every time he said a word," Tony said, still smarting from the fact that the girl Alan was feeling up was from Jersey.

"Maybe being funny makes women hot," Jon suggested.

"I can do a Henny Youngman impression: 'Take my wife … please,'" Tony said, displaying a terrible Henny Youngman voice.

"Yeah, I can tell *that* impression will sure as hell get you laid," Augie said as he rolled his eyes.

Tony slugged Augie in the arm and got slugged back.

> JT — A couple of nights later, Augie, Tony, and I were just leaving the Midwest Theater when we saw Alan and three girls walking ahead of us on Broadway. Every few feet, they would stop, and the girls would take turns kissing Alan while the other two would rub his back or shoulders. Our individual and group jealousy was palpable. Then Tony noticed that one of the girls handed Alan a wad of cash.

"You guys see that? That little fucker is doing the same work for those girls as he is for the basketball team. He's not only making money, but he's also probably getting laid. What a racket."

"Imagine the cash we could make with our looks if we were smart," Augie lamented.

"Guy must be making a fortune," Tony said.

"He is a pretty smart guy. I saw he aced that Bio quiz last week," Jon noted.

"And the Western Civ midterm too," Augie reported.

As depression set in for Tony, he said, "You know, I don't think the girls out here in farm country dig me."

"Hell, most of the girls out here are from Jersey, Philly, and New York. They don't dig you because you're just an ugly butthole and get C's in Bio."

"Fuck you, dick breath, I look just like you."

"Bullshit. Our hair is different, and your face looks like my ass."

With no further comment the brothers began pounding each other but with no head shots, an event Jon had become used to.

JT — When I saw the brothers begin to square off, I usually just walked on ahead of them and let them duke it out, or I sat down somewhere and watched the show until they got tired.

As the year wore on, we got into some habits that included watching certain TV shows at night, like *The Man from U.N.C.L.E.*, *I Spy*, *The Wild, Wild West* or any show or black-and-white movie that was about guys fighting in a war—any war. Tony loved those shows and would react like a ten-year-old when a US Marine would lay waste to a group of bad guys, usually Asian or German, with a machine gun. The more dead bad guys the better.

On a Friday night, in their dorm room Tony, Augie, and Jon ate pizza and watched John Wayne kill people. A lot of people.

"Next year at this time, I'll be in the Green Berets, and I'll be doing all that stuff John Wayne does," Tony said as he mentally counted the days and potential Viet Cong bodies.

"You do realize that is just a movie, right, and he's not really killing real people?" Jon pointed out.

"Yeah, but that shit really happens."

"You're gonna go over there and get your ass shot and come home in a body bag. Besides, what have those people done to you?" Augie asked.

"They're all commies; they're born that way. We gotta kill them over there before they come over here and kill us," Tony informed.

"That's bullshit. What do you think of the war, Jon?"

"I know for sure you can get your ass killed in Nam. A few of my friends never made it back in one piece."

"We had a few guys killed from our class too, but my dipshit brother thinks war is cool," Augie said.

"You guys are just pussies," Tony said dismissively.

"And you're a dumb fuck who's gonna go over there, last a week, and get your fucking empty head blown off," Augie responded.

"You're the dumb fuck." Tony said as he rose to take on his pussy brother, but a knock on the door distracted his attention.

CHAPTER 12

CHRYSLER DEATH SPIRAL

"Go away, no one is here. Besides, we're watching TV," Tony demanded.

From the other side of the door, a familiar voice. "It's me, Alan. You guys wanna go on a picnic?"

"It's almost dark, you crazy fucker," Augie yelled.

"We got beer, food, music, and girls," Alan said calmly.

As one, and without saying a word, Augie, Tony, and Jon rose off the couch and exited their room. Alan led them downstairs to an old 1953 Chrysler New Yorker sedan parked at the curb. Around it, four girls lounged on the fenders of the behemoth, while two guys loaded beer and food.

"Where the hell did you find this old piece of crap?" Jon asked Alan.

"I bought it from a guy at the Esso last week for fifty bucks."

"Does it run?"

"Of course it runs, and it's got enough gas to get us out to the monument and back. The basketball team invited me and a bunch of other people. They told me to bring some beer and food. Let's go!"

The group of ten crammed into the huge sedan with the girls sitting on the guys' laps. The radio found an AM station, and the group sang "Stop in the Name of Love" by the Supremes, along with several other Top Forty hits on our trip to a bluff.

Jon sat in the middle front seat as Alan drove and Augie rode shotgun. Despite the music and off-key singing, Jon heard some ominous sounds coming from the engine. "Think this thing will make it?" he asked Alan.

"What's the probability that this twelve-year-old car with over 100,000 miles will pick this very night, in its long career of faithfully serving mankind, to die? I mean, what are the odds statistically?"

Since he had gotten A's in Statistics in high school, Jon replied, "From the sounds of this thing's engine, I'd say the odds are pretty fucking good."

As the Chrysler chugged out of town, leaving behind a gray line of exhaust, the sun was setting on the Scotts Bluff National Monument ten miles in the distance. The bluff was bathed in changing hues of tans, purples, browns, and grays.

> JT — I remember thinking that night that it was the first time I had actually seen the Scotts Bluff Monument at that time of the day, and I was taken by how beautiful it was. Despite everyone singing "Louie, Louie" at the top of their lungs, I kept staring at the bluff as we got closer and closer, and the emptiness of the surrounding landscape made me feel a loneliness that was not at all explainable, given I was in a 1953 Chrysler with nine other people who were singing rock-and-roll songs. I think it was that the beauty I was witnessing was the kind of thing you wanted to share with someone special. For some reason, I thought Anna would have enjoyed looking at that damn bluff, and I badly missed a girl I had only spent five minutes of face-to-face time with.

At the top of the bluff, the students wore jackets and sweaters as a cool, stiff wind blew across the monument. Everyone had gathered wood and started a huge fire that kept people semi-warm.

Car doors were left open, and radios tuned to the same station to provide an early version of surround sound. Two beer kegs were set up, and red wine bottles were passed around the group. Hot dogs were cooked over the fire, and couples paired off under blankets and stared up at an array of stars that could never have been seen as clearly from their large, smog-covered cities back home.

On one side of the fire, Jon and Jimmy sat on the ground, drinking beers and staring into the flames.

"You miss Philly?" Jon asked.

"Sure, lived there all my life. Really miss my ma. She's all alone now after my dad left and one of my brothers got killed in Nam."

"Oh my God, I'm sorry, man."

"Thanks. I had two older brothers, and they had enlisted together. After the one got killed, my other brother deserted and moved to Canada since he didn't want my mom to lose another son over there. We ain't heard from him for over a year, for fear he could be tracked down and sent to prison."

"Maybe when the war is over …" Jon suggested.

"Yeah, maybe he'll come back then. Funny thing was my ma never cried when she heard Billy had been killed, at least not in front of me. It's like she kept everything inside, and I think it's eating her up. I was too tall to get drafted, but I had made her a solemn promise I'd get a college degree from somewhere before I go pro. So here I am. Where are you from?"

"San Diego."

"Nice there?"

"Yeah, but I don't want to spend the rest of my life there."

"Why not? It's home."

"I want to head back East to a big city. Big cities sound exciting."

"Yeah, Philly, New York, and DC are cool. Lots to do, good food and music. How the hell did you end up out here? You sound like a smart guy."

"Long story short, I got my girlfriend pregnant, at least I thought I did, but when I found out the truth that she wasn't, it was too late to go anywhere else."

"That's a pisser."

"Jimmy, is it true … what I mean is … did you really …?"

"Yeah, I mooned the coach's wife and got kicked out of Villanova."

"That's a pisser too. Guys on the team say you're good enough to make it to the NBA."

"Maybe, but me exposing my black ass has cooled interest with some of the teams that were talking to me. At least for now. But if I have a good year this season, things should work out."

"Why did you …?"

"Why did I do it? No damn clue, man. It was a spur-of-the-moment thing. If those women hadn't got off that elevator at that very moment or I had gone into my room ten seconds before I did, I'd be back in Philly right now."

"Damn, it's amazing how one little thing you do can mess up everything."

Jimmy and Jon continued to stare into the fire and sat silently for several minutes as music and laughter surrounded them.

"Where were you going to school before the unpregnant girlfriend?"

"Annapolis."

"Why'd you pick that place, you want to be a warlord or something?"

"You don't pick the Naval Academy, they pick you. It's called an appointment. But I always thought about going there. Guess it was because I lived in San Diego and used to see all those ships going in and out of there for years. I thought that was cool. And if I went there, it would be a free education." Jon replied.

"So, I was right, you are smart."

"Not very. I never confirmed my girlfriend was pregnant."

Jimmy laughed out loud at Jon's self-appraisal.

"Well, I know I'm not that smart, never really liked school, just loved playing basketball. It's my thing, ya know. It was something I could do better than most guys. It gave me a rep. Everybody in Philly knew me. I hit the books just hard enough to stay eligible, and there were always professors around that gave the players the grades if we needed it."

"Why did you come out here to farmland?"

"Not many schools would touch me after what happened, and Coach Anderson has a great reputation and told me he knew lots of scouts, and if I did well, he'd see to it I'd get my shot."

"Is it true he got fired at Michigan State?"

"Yeah, I heard it was over some bullshit college politics. Maybe that's why he gave me a second chance. Maybe this place is a second chance for him too."

Jimmy and Jon looked over at Alan, who was talking to several girls around the fire, one of whom was under a blanket with him.

"Alan there is a real trip. Funny guy, pretty smart too," Jon said.

"Yeah, he's keeping most of us eligible with his tutoring."

"Yeah, with what you guys and those girls we see him with all the time are paying him for tutoring, he must be making a bundle off his brains."

"It ain't his brains those girls are paying him for."

"What do you mean?" Jon asked.

"You mean you don't know about Big Al?"

"Know what?" Jon asked.

"That skinny little white boy over there has a ten-inch schlong."

"What? That's bullshit!"

"No lie. One night, he came into the locker room after a game to shower up before he went out that night with the team, and he turned that big ole one-eyed albino python loose. I swear every Black guy in that locker room took notice. It's a monster. That man got instant respect."

"Ten inches!?"

"At least. That damn thing is somethin' else. Never knew white guys could have that kind of ammunition," Jimmy said with sincere admiration.

"Holy shit. So that's why …"

"Hell, when those girls found out about ol' Alan's love unit, they at least wanted to see that damn thing, so he started charging to give them a look-see. Not all of them wanted to take on that monster up close and personal, although I heard some did have the courage, but all of them sure as hell wanted to see it."

"I'll be damned. Alan sure is full of surprises."

Jimmy and Jon looked over at Alan. He had a girl on each side of him under a blanket; all three people were smiling.

At around 2 a.m., the fires had burned down to ashes, and it was getting colder by the minute. Jon, Alan, Tony, Augie, and the six others who had driven out with them earlier in the evening decided it was time to head back to town.

When Alan turned the key in the ignition, there was nothing but that dreaded, internationally known clicking sound from under the hood.

"Damn, I think the battery is dead," Alan announced.

"No shit, Sherlock. We better let someone know before we're stranded on top of this damn rock all night," Tony said.

"Maybe someone has jumper cables," Augie said.

"Screw it, let's push it off," Alan said nonchalantly.

"What do you mean?" Jon asked, hoping he understood what Alan was thinking.

"Hell, it only cost fifty bucks. I'll make that much tomorrow from the team. Besides, it would be a cool thing to see."

Tony loved that plan. "Fuck yeah, let's push this old piece of shit off this rock. That would be cool as hell."

Augie ran to tell the rest of the group about Alan's demolition plans. He returned with five guys, all willing to help in any possible form of mindless destruction.

Alan addressed the group. "Okay, guys, before we do this, I think someone with a religious connection needs to say a little prayer. A 1953 Chrysler New Yorker prayer, in order to save this noble sedan's metallic soul."

After several minutes of silence, Gus Pappas, a young man from Boston, stepped forward. "Well, my cousin dated a woman whose brother was almost a priest until he got caught screwing a nurse who was also a stripper, so I guess you could say I have a religious connection."

"That's close enough for me. Have at it, Father Gus," Alan said.

JT — Gus was a very short, very good-looking, dark-haired guy who hardly ever said a word. Yet it seemed he was always around when we did stuff. He'd always come to games, or movies with the group, and even the parties, but he never had much to say. He would just sit there and laugh at all the crazy shit that went down. That's why it was kind of weird when quiet little Gus volunteered to lead this solemn religious ceremony bidding farewell to a 1953 Chrysler. Later he said it was "beer courage."

As the crowd gathered around the condemned Chrysler, someone started to hum the "Battle Hymn of the Republic." Pretty soon everyone joined in, and the humming echoed off the rock walls and encouraged everyone to move closer and lay their hands on the soon-to-be deader-than-hell Detroit creation. With the somber humming in the background, Gus placed his hands on the car's back right fender.

"Lord, we are about to return to you a beat-to-shit 1953 Chrysler New Yorker that rode okay but smelled a little like piss. If you are a Cadillac or Oldsmobile guy, we hope you are not offended by our offering, but it's all we have except for my 1963 Corvette Sting Ray split window with a four speed and Positraction, which I am not giving up for anything except maybe a naked Sophia Loren delivered to my room along with some serious cash. Sorry, no checks. Please accept this offering, and if you want to join us for a last beer, that would be cool. Amen."

The rest of the group joined in with a resounding "AMEN."

Two guys got behind the New Yorker and began to push, but more muscle was needed to move the massive car. Soon over a dozen guys and girls got behind the behemoth and pushed.

The wheels reluctantly turned and made a distinctive crunching sound as they slowly moved over the rocks and dirt. The condemned former luxury sedan picked up speed as it headed toward the black abyss, and as the students moved out of the way, the laughter began. Then there was silence when the pride of Detroit became airborne.

JT — While I had forgotten the precise equation for how quickly a free-falling object obtains terminal velocity (I seem to recall it took something like twelve seconds and 1,500 feet), given the time lapse from when the Chrysler was pushed into space until the time it hit, that son of a bitch was moving faster than it ever had on a road. When the three-ton metal monster finally hit the ground, the sound was like a muffled bomb that kept reverberating as the car bounced off rock and rolled over several times, while metal crunched and glass broke. It was a beautiful thing.

The sheer audacity of buying a car, even a $50 car, filling it with beer, driving it to the top of a bluff, playing its radio until the battery went dead, and then pushing it off that bluff was something we all saw as a definitive and even required path into adulthood.

By the time Tony, Augie, and I got back to our dorm, it was nearly 5 a.m., and we were all tired, but that night was a memory none of us would ever forget.

There was a surrealness about it that was heightened by a lot of beer, a high altitude, and bonding with new friends, like Gus. A big part of that memory was also having an opportunity to get to know Jimmy better. He was always a friendly guy around campus who would smile and say hi, but getting to know him on a deeper level was enlightening. I liked the guy. He was not just friendly with a big smile; he was intelligent, humble, and thoughtful. Plus, given I was sure he would become an NBA star someday, I saw some free Laker tickets in my future.

Chapter 13

Hawk vs. Dove

JT — I usually ate a cheap breakfast of toast and coffee at the Eagle Café, and from there, I could see a slice of Scottsbluff's everyday life and the Hiram Scott students' *interesting* behaviors. On several occasions, I would smile when I saw Jimmy and Gus walk by the window, laughing and giving each other some grief. They were an odd pair, to be sure, since Jimmy was 6'8" and Gus was, on a good day, maybe 5'6", but they had become best friends, and it seemed both had come out of their shells as the school year wore on.

Of course, I would also see Tony and Augie hit on every girl within two blocks, although it eventually dawned on me that I never saw either one of them on a date. I doubted either was gay, but I wondered what would happen if one of those girls they hit on would actually take them up on a proposition and say, "Okay, let's go to your room and get it on, stud."

While eating my favored pancakes, I could also see the new army recruiter trying to get every guy who passed him to sign up and visit downtown Hanoi. I remember wanting to shout out, "Don't do it" to the guys I saw follow that recruiter back into his office. I often wondered how many of those guys came back in body bags and if that recruiter ever cared.

One Saturday morning, while eating waffles and sausage, I noticed what, at first, was a small group of townies and students gathered in front of the army recruiting office. Each group carried signs indicating the strong opposition to or support of the expanding conflict, now officially the Vietnam War.

The groups initially engaged in what I would call an "earnest conversation." But things suddenly turned physical when a former Korean War vet used his sign as a club and hit a student in the head with his "Stop the Commies" sign. That move caused the students to attack the townies with their own signs, beer bottles, and anything else they could find, and within minutes, a full-fledged melee was under way, which led to some broken noses, a couple of concussions, some black eyes, and assorted cuts and bruises that were relatively minor short-term injuries, and arrests.

What was more long term, and far more disturbing, was the fact that the town was now openly divided, and a clear line had been drawn between pro-war and anti-war factions. These differences replaced the seemingly mutual acceptance that had existed between the groups when school had started.

As a result, a simmering undercurrent of resentment and distrust was never far from the surface, which included the veiled threat of even more and possibly increased violence between local citizens and the students.

While there were some townies who, like the students, opposed the war, and even some students who supported it, it appeared that literal battlelines had now been drawn in front of that office, and what was happening in the small town of Scottsbluff, Nebraska, had become a microcosm of what was happening in the large cities all around the country.

After the first couple of months, we had all gotten into a routine, met friends we wanted to hang out with, and settled down to what would be our lives at least until the end of that first school year the following June.

The citizens of Scottsbluff were getting used to the influx of students and faculty who were "different" beyond just the war. The residents also got used to an occasional fight on a street corner, usually Tony and Augie, more traffic, more crowds at restaurants, but all in all, most saw the college and its students as a plus for the town.

People also got behind the basketball team and filled the stands every time it played and the fact it kicked the snot out of most of the teams it played given the roster of former high school and college All-Americans Forddy Anderson had assembled.

The people in town also took a liking to "that Black guy" as they referred to Jimmy, and he became a fan favorite and would sign dozens of autographs every time he was out to dinner.

Given my limited financial resources, I decided I could not afford to go home for Christmas. Well, the truth is I was planning to come home mainly to see Anna, but she told me her parents were taking the family to Hawaii for the holidays, and she would not be there. So, I decided to save my money and fly back to see her over a long weekend during the long Nebraska winter.

I was at first hesitant to write to Anna because I wasn't sure she really wanted me to write to her, and maybe she was just feeling sorry for me that day I was leaving.

Then a week later, she wrote to me, telling me I was a jerk for not writing to her like I said I would. She wondered if I had fallen in love with someone else already. From that point on, we wrote every week. Actually, she wrote every day, and I wrote every week.

Since I had the time in the dorm, which was virtually empty over the Christmas break, I decided to organize my journal, which I had started back in San Diego. But my butt was sore from sitting all day, and I was tired of writing. So, I decided to go for a walk in the snow that had started falling a few hours earlier. Walking in snow was something I had never done before, and I felt the time was right.

CHAPTER 14

MERRY CHRISTMAS: 1965

Jon walked alone on Broadway in what began as light snow and peered into the closed shops. He wore a winter coat with a hood pulled over his head, hands in his pockets since he forgot he might need gloves in Nebraska in the winter and didn't pack any. At one point he looked straight up into the sky and opened his mouth and wondered if snow had a taste. It didn't.

With most of the students gone and most townies at home on Christmas Eve, he had virtually the entire town to himself, except there was nothing to do in town. Even the Midwest movie theater was closed.

When he approached a street corner, a family of four waited for the light to change, even though there were absolutely no cars on the street. At first, he thought about walking around the family but figured that would be bad form in Scottsbluff.

As he waited for the green light, Jon turned and smiled at the family. They all smiled back. The mother had a question. "You a Scottie?"

"Yes, ma'am, I go to Hiram Scott."

"You from here? You don't look familiar."

"No, ma'am, I'm from California."

The mother was a tall, slender woman named Ellen. She had been born in Denver but moved to Scottsbluff with her family when she was ten. Her face showed no signs of makeup but was handsome and healthy. And pretty.

Her husband, Carl, was a large, gruff-looking man who wore heavy wool pants and a drab, worn wool coat with a combination of white paint and mud on it.

The kids—Ethan was twelve and Nan was almost eight—wore stylish, matching ski jackets, boots, wool hats, and leather gloves.

"Didn't go home for Christmas?" Ellen asked.

"Didn't have the time."

"No time for family on Christmas?"

"It was a money thing too."

"I can understand that." Carl said knowingly.

When the light changed, the newly formed group of five crossed the street and walked down Broadway.

"That's too bad. People need to be with family over Christmas."

"Yes, ma'am."

"He said it was a time and money thing, Ellen. Let the boy be."

Ellen ignored Carl. "I'll bet your folks are missing you."

"I'll call them tomorrow."

"Not the same. You know all the restaurants will be closed here in town on Christmas day."

"Oh, I'll be fine. I have some stuff in our dorm room. We have a small fridge in there."

Nan, the daughter, looked up at Jon. "I'm Nan Walker, I'm eight, almost, and I don't believe in Santa Claus. Never did."

"Really?"

"Yeah, all the kids at school do, but they're stupid. I mean, the idea of a Santa Claus is also kinda stupid if you ask me," Nan said with conviction.

"Did it bother you when you found out there was no Santa?" Jon asked.

"A little at first, but like I said, it made no sense. Did it bother you when you found out?"

"Yeah, it did."

"Really?"

"I was about your age and remember thinking everyone had lied to me for a long time, and I felt a little betrayed. You know what betrayed means?"

"Screwed?"

Jon laughed at her answer. "Yeah, kinda screwed."

"I felt bad for a while but figured Mom and Dad were kinda Santa Claus in a way, so I went with it."

"What about the Easter Bunny?"

"I thought he was crap when I was five."

"Yeah, I never bought into that big bunny thing either."

Jon and the Walker family came to another red light and stopped. "Well, it was nice talking to you folks. I'm going to head back to the dorm. You all have a Merry Christmas."

Jon turned to cross the street when he heard Carl's voice. "Hey, boy."

Jon stopped and turned back toward Carl. "Yes, sir?"

"We're havin' Christmas dinner tomorrow at our house with all the trimmin's, and if you want to come join us, you're welcome."

"Well, sir, that's very nice of you, but I wouldn't want to interfere with your family …"

"If I thought you'd be interferin', I wouldn'a asked ya."

"My mom makes a really good turkey," Nan said.

"Good pumpkin pie too," Ethan volunteered.

> JT — After I accepted Mr. Walker's dinner invitation, I had to admit a turkey dinner sounded great. I got their address, and they told me to show up the next day around noon.

> As we all said goodbye, heavy snow began to fall, and suddenly, things felt like Christmas—the kind of Christmas people from California see on old TV shows and movies. The kind of Christmas we never see in Southern California.

> There was also a total quiet in the deserted town that was only interrupted by my feet crunching through snow, which now fell at a blinding rate.

By the time I had made it back to the dorm, two to three inches had already fallen, and while I was cold, I sat outside on the steps and let the snow cover me like I was a statue. Not sure why I did that but after never experiencing snow before, I wanted to savor the experience. After twenty minutes or so, I had savored enough and was freezing my ass off. I decided I wanted to go inside and write Anna a letter and tell her about my Christmas dinner invitation.

After writing to Anna, I thought about not showing up the next day at the Walkers, fearing I'd mess up their family dinner. But I wondered how many other families would've been willing to invite a perfect stranger off the street into their house after a ten-minute conversation.

Later I learned that several folks in Scottsbluff did kind of adopt many of the Scotties, thinking they could use a good meal from time to time, including Christmas dinners. I guess they felt kind of sorry for some of us and were maybe a bit curious too. In my case, I finally decided it would be rude not to go. Pumpkin pie was also a deciding factor.

The next morning, Jon followed the directions he had been given the night before and walked a mile in what had become foot-deep snow to the neighborhood where the Walkers lived. The bright sunshine that reflected off the snow made him appreciate the sunglasses he had brought from California. He had also worn the first pair of rubber boots he had ever owned, which he had a hell of a time putting on but was now glad he had.

On his walk, he saw the houses and trees covered in deep, fluffy snow and was reminded of a Norman Rockwell painting he had seen on a *Saturday Evening Post* magazine cover years before.

The houses he passed were small and neat, and smoke curled from many of their chimneys. He could see Christmas trees shining brightly through many windows, and everyone he passed on the street smiled and wished him a Merry Christmas.

When he turned the corner that led to the Walkers' home, he noticed it was considerably larger than most of the other houses he had passed. It was a brick Craftsman-style house with wood trim and a large veranda-type front porch that nearly encircled the entire home. It also had a huge backyard with tall oak and ash trees, with a detached three-car garage behind the house.

> JT — When I knocked on the front door, I heard a barking dog and, within seconds, saw the face of a large brown mixed breed, who I later learned was Ike.
>
> After Nan opened the door, greeted me, and again reminded me she did not believe in Santa Claus, Ike sniffed me a few times, then licked my face when I knelt to pet him. His job complete, he lay back down in front of a fireplace that crackled and produced serious heat, and he fell asleep for several hours.

"Hey, Mom, Jon's here," Nan announced.

"Take his coat and show him where the bathroom is, just in case," Ellen said from the kitchen.

Nan hung his coat in the closet and pointed to the bathroom door. "There's the toilet. No one can use that one, so it stays clean for company like you."

"Thanks. I promise to keep it clean."

When Jon looked around the living room, he saw a huge Christmas tree in the corner. It had multicolored lights and ornaments along with small artificial birds, squirrels, and chipmunks scattered among the limbs. Icicle-type garland was all over the tree, and the ten-foot Scottish pine was topped off with a large white angel.

"Wow, that's quite a tree," Jon said to Nan.

"Yeah, Mom goes a little crazy when it comes to decorating for Christmas."

Jon also saw a large fireplace with seven stockings that hung from a thick oak hearth.

> JT — While I looked at that large tree, it dawned on me that I was also engulfed in the aroma of roasted turkey, sage dressing, gravy, and baking Parker House dinner rolls. The look of the tree and avalanche

of aromas from the food emanating from the kitchen confirmed I had made a wise decision to join the Walkers for dinner.

"Jon, do you *wanna* see what I got for Christmas?" Nan asked.

"Sure."

Nan ran, then slid on her knees toward the tree and carefully pulled out her new chemistry set. "I'm gonna be a doctor someday, so I told Mom I needed to get started right away."

"No use wasting time. What kind of doctor?"

"A head doctor. You know, fix people's brains. A neurosurgeon."

"I think I could use some help in that area."

When Ellen entered the living room from the kitchen, she smiled as she wiped her hands on her apron. She also had a quarter-size touch of flour on her chin. "Hi, Jon, we're so glad you came. We were afraid you might change your mind. Ethan and Carl are out back getting more firewood. We'll be ready to eat in a few minutes, though."

"Thanks again for asking me. It sure smells good in here."

"I helped with the mashed potatoes, even though I hate mashed potatoes. Felt it was the right thing to do," Nan volunteered.

"Definitely the right thing to do. And don't worry, I'll eat your share," Jon volunteered back.

"Good, glad somebody will."

> JT — After we finally sat down and began to destroy a fourteen-pound turkey, I could not help but notice the easy back-and-forth of the conversation. Ellen and Carl engaged Nan and Ethan in adult conversation and did not talk down to them. In return, the kids were polite and said "please" and "thank you" when asking for more gravy or dressing. They also engaged me.

"You miss California?" Ellen asked.

"I miss the weather, but I'm anxious to go back East after this year."

"Staying in Scottsbluff for just a year?" Carl asked.

"That's the plan, but I've learned not all plans work out the way you think they will."

"What do you want to do when you're through with school?" Ellen asked.

"Not sure, maybe a professor or a writer, or both."

"What do you want to write about?" Nan asked.

"People."

"That subject will give you lots of options," Ellen observed.

"I'd write about the brain and tell people everything I've learned in college so doctors can fix broken brains," Nan said.

Ethan announced, "I'm going to be a lawyer when I grow up and be on the United States Supreme Court."

"Before you all become writers, doctors, and lawyers, how about some pumpkin pie?" Ellen suggested.

> JT — As everyone loosened up, our conversations over dessert covered a wide range of topics, including The Beatles, Rolling Stones, James Bond movies, a boy in Nan's class she said had a crush on her and she hated, and Ethan's contention that there had been at least two shooters in Dallas.

Not wanting to wear out his welcome, Jon said, "Folks, that was a great dinner. Thanks again for inviting me today."

"No one should be alone on Christmas," Ellen said.

"I guess even the guys in Vietnam get turkey and dressing on Christmas. I saw on TV how helicopters deliver all the food behind the lines," Jon said.

After several moments of silence, Carl asked a pointed question. "You in college just to get out of the draft?"

"Carl, no talk of that war at Christmas dinner," Ellen said softly.

Carl replied, "Just a simple question. I see all those students around the country on TV burning their draft cards, protesting in the street, even here in town, and just wanted to know how Jon here feels about all that stuff and the war."

Jon felt uncomfortable but looked directly at Carl and answered his question. "I don't like this war or any war. Lots of people get killed, and nothing ever seems to be solved by all that death and destruction. But I don't have the guts to move to Canada or burn my draft card. The guys who do are the brave ones because they are saying no to the government and what appears to be an illegal war."

Carl pushed the issue. "What if all the boys said no and moved to Canada? What then, Jon?"

"Then I guess all the politicians who start the wars would have to go fight them."

For several moments, Carl and Jon stared at each other. Finally, Ellen had a suggestion. "C'mon, everyone, let's go into the living room and see what Santa left in everyone's stocking."

As the group walked into the living room, Nan sidled up to Jon and said, "Mom likes to keep that Santa thing going. Makes her feel good, so I let it go."

"That's a good idea on your part," Jon agreed.

> JT — Over the next hour, we all talked, laughed, and looked into our stockings, including Ike, who got a big leather bone, which he immediately began to gnaw on the hardwood floor. I felt bad they'd given me a pair of hand-made woolen gloves because I had not brought anything for any of them.

> Ethan had received a small Polaroid camera and was taking endless pictures using popping flashcubes that temporarily blinded us.

"Okay, Ethan, enough pictures," Carl said.

> JT — After all of us had gotten our stockings, I noticed there was one that remained hanging on the fireplace mantel. "Who got left out?" I asked.

For several moments there was silence in the room. Finally, Nan said, "That stocking is for my older brother, Michael. He was killed in a helicopter crash in Vietnam last year. He was twenty-five years old and a pilot. He was a cool guy and a good brother."

JT — I felt like total shit. The rest of the family just sat there and looked at the stocking. I tried to think of something to say, but whatever I would have come up with would have only made things worse if that was even possible. So, I just sat there like the fucking idiot I was.

In fact, over the next few minutes, we all just sat there, knowing there was no right thing to say. There was nothing anyone could say that would make anyone feel the least bit better. A son, and a brother, who was deeply loved by his family, was dead. Dead because of a fucking war in a place few people had ever heard of. Dead because politicians in Washington figured we could afford to lose a certain number of young men, so long as those losses were "acceptable," which meant we killed more Viet Cong than they killed American boys.

As I sat there in that awful silence, I wished those who started that war would be forced to attend a Christmas dinner when a family dealt with an empty stocking on a fireplace. I could almost feel the grief as it invaded the room and brought with it a sense of loss that was palpable and total.

With no words being said, Nan and Ellen eventually went to the dining room table and began to take the dirty dishes out into the kitchen.

Carl went back outside for more firewood, and Ethan went to his room and took more pictures. After a few minutes, I went to the kitchen and was tasked with drying the dishes along with Nan, but she soon left to make new discoveries with her chemistry set.

"I'm so sorry I brought up … " Jon said while drying a dinner plate.

"Don't worry yourself, Jon. How could you know? It's our first Christmas without Michael, and we all knew it was going to be rough on all of us."

After the dishes were done, Ellen and Jon sat at the kitchen table and drank hot tea. Through the window they could see Carl pacing across the yard with his head down and his hands in his pockets.

"Carl was the only one of us who never cried when we got word about Michael. I wish he had. I think he would have been better by now, but I guess none of us will ever really be better. I just wish the pain would go away," Ellen said softly.

"Was he drafted?"

"No, he enlisted. Michael always wanted to be a pilot and even got his flying license when he was sixteen. He was crop-dusting out here by the time he was eighteen. When he came to us and said he wanted to go over there, he told us, and we believed, the United States was just going to be advisors, so we never thought Michael would be in any real danger. In fact, Carl believed everything he heard from Washington and the President and told Michael to go over there, learn to fly, then come home and become an airline pilot. That's why Carl feels so much guilt, because he encouraged Michael to enlist."

"How did it happen?"

"He was flying some Army brass in a Huey, and they were hit by machine gun fire. Michael was shot in the head but managed to land the chopper and survive the crash but died later in a field hospital. The survivors said Michael saved their lives."

"Is that why Nan …?"

"She says she could have fixed his brain and saved Michael if she had been there."

> JT — For the next thirty minutes, Mrs. Walker and I talked. She was as nice a person as I had ever met. But she was also bright, witty, and knew things. She told me that next Christmas I needed to be home with my family for the holidays, and I promised I would. Before I left, she returned from the kitchen and carried a brown paper bag.

"I packed you a little mess kit of turkey, mashed potatoes, and dressing so you'll have something to eat tomorrow," Ellen said.

"Thank you. I know what I'll have for dinner tomorrow now. I always enjoyed warmed-up turkey after a Christmas dinner."

> JT — At her front door, Mrs. Walker hugged me and made sure I had not forgotten my new wool gloves. I hugged her back, thanked her again for the gloves, and told her those were the first pair I had ever owned and promised I would take good care of them.

After waving goodbye to Ellen, Nan, and Ethan from the front porch, Jon walked down the front porch stairs and saw Carl still walking aimlessly in the backyard with his head down. Jon walked toward him. "Mr. Walker, before I left, I wanted to thank you for inviting me to dinner today. I appreciate it."

"You're welcome. Looked like you enjoyed that turkey."

"Yes, sir, I did."

Jon fell into step with Carl, and they began walking around the yard side by side. For several moments neither spoke. Finally, they began to talk about football, then baseball; then, out of nowhere, Carl said, "I was the one who encouraged Michael to go over there. Ellen said it would be too dangerous, but I told her she was being silly and not giving Michael a chance to do what he wanted to do. It was just two years ago around this time that he left, and it wasn't really even a war then … It was … something else. Had I known …"

"The government lied to all of us, Mr. Walker."

"Yeah, I guess it did. It's taken me some time to admit that to myself, but I served in World War II, and we all enlisted; it was just expected. We all wanted to go and fight and defend our country, and we never thought our country would lie to us back then."

While the men walked, snow began falling again, and the darkness made the cold seem deeper and more penetrating, like some memories.

"I had some friends who never came back alive from Nam. I'm afraid many, many more will go over there, and they won't come back alive either," Jon said.

"Like I said, I never thought our country would lie to us like that. When I started to see all the protests on TV, especially after Mikey was killed, I hated all you kids with your signs and long hair."

"My mom hates my long hair too."

Carl turned, shot a glance at Jon. "At least yours is clean."

"I shower every day," Jon said with a small grin.

Carl smiled back. "I sure miss that boy."

"I'm very sorry."

"I've got to go on for Ellen and the kids. By the way, my little pistol, Nan, really likes you. She really misses Mikey too."

"I can tell. She's a trip and very smart."

"Takes after her mom."

The men stopped near the front of the garage and talked face-to-face.

"You like cars?" Carl asked.

"Sure."

Carl moved to one of the garage doors and lifted it. He reached over and turned on a light. Inside was the outline of a car covered with several blankets. One by one Carl removed them and exposed a shiny piece of automotive art; it was a black 1949 Cadillac convertible with a red and black leather interior. It also had a Continental kit. The wire wheels had been custom made, along with the wide whitewall tires.

"Oh my God, that thing is gorgeous," Jon gasped.

Carl smiled and said, "Michael bought it five years ago, and it was a piece of junk. We'd come out here and work on it almost every night. Do a little at a time. Slowly, we rebuilt it."

"How's she run?"

"Don't know. Mikey and I agreed we'd wait to take it for its maiden run when he got home but …"

As he spoke, Carl rubbed his hands over the deep red leather front seat of the car. "He picked out this leather and rebuilt the interior from the ground up. I remember we had a hell of a time putting these things in, but it was worth it."

"What engine?"

"Overhead valve Cadillac 331, but we did a little stroke and bore and think she runs around 385 horses now. We were gonna go with two four barrels when he got back. I got them sitting in a box over there." Carl stroked the red leather seat again.

"You guys did a beautiful job; you should be really proud of that."

"Thanks, I am." Carl re-covered the Caddy, turned out the light, and the men left the garage.

"Thanks again for the invite today. Hope I didn't eat too much."

"You're welcome. We'll do it again as long as you keep your hair clean."

"That's a deal. See ya later."

"See ya."

Jon waved goodbye and started to walk away, then stopped and turned back toward Carl, who was still on the porch. "Mr. Walker?"

"Yeah?"

"Mr. Walker, I never knew Michael, but if my dad and I ever built a car like that and I wasn't around anymore, I'd sure hope he'd take that car for rides all the time. And even if he couldn't see me, I'd somehow let him know I was sitting there right next to him."

Carl did not respond to Jon, but instead slowly nodded his head and waved to Jon, who waved back.

As the winter sun set just after five, Jon walked back to his dorm, his new rubber boots crunching through the freezing snow.

JT — The Walkers were the third family I had met in less than a year who had been devastated after losing a son in Vietnam. Even though it was eighteen degrees, and I was walking through what was now over a foot of snow in a small corner of Nebraska over eight thousand miles away from Saigon, that war in the jungle seemed to be getting closer and closer each day.

I ended up visiting the Walkers a bunch of times while I was in Scottsbluff. I was invited to several dinners, and we would discuss world events, including the war. Mr. Walker even erected a "STOP the WAR" sign in his front yard.

I would also visit with Ethan and Nan, and they would ask questions about … well … questions about everything. Nan would show me her latest experiments with her chemistry set, while Ethan would want to discuss what law school he should attend.

We also talked a lot about Nebraska football and basketball. Ethan was particularly grateful when I took him for lunch downtown, and we had a hamburger with Jimmy. Ethan had never even spoken to a

Black man before, let alone one 6'8". "Are all Black people that tall?" he had asked. Later that night, I showed him a picture of Sammy Davis Jr.

I also stayed in touch with them after college, but we never talked about the war again. It was just too painful.

That spring, Tony, Augie, Gus, Jimmy, Alan, and I were just coming out of the bakery, prepared to overload on a bag of warm glazed donuts, when Tony said, "Holy shit, look at that fucking car." We all looked up and saw Mr. Walker driving down Broadway in a black Cadillac with a rolled and pleated red leather interior. Its top was down, and the radio was playing "Satisfaction" by the Stones. You could also hear the threatening rumble of two four-barrel carburetors. As he turned the corner to head out of town, I remember thinking that even with all visual evidence to the contrary, he was not alone.

CHAPTER 15

SECOND TRIMESTER

JT — After everyone came back from Christmas break, we soon returned to our regular routine and were hopeful that President Johnson's stopping of the bombing in North Vietnam was a precursor to the war finally ending. It did not end. It expanded.

Of course, Tony was counting the days until he could finally enlist, and he hoped the war did not end before he had his chance to "kill me some commies." He got further amped up every time he heard the "Ballad of the Green Berets" recorded by Staff Sergeant Barry Sadler. Everywhere he went in town, Tony would sing that damn song. Actually, he got pretty good at it.

On a Saturday in late January, Augie entered the dorm room and sank down on the couch next to Jon and watched NBC Saturday News and saw the now familiar news footage of B-52s making bombing runs over North Vietnam. It had become a repeated scene on national TV.

Between sips of beer a glum Augie said, "There was another 'Greetings from the President' letter today. Greg, down the hall, got his notice … His GPA dropped below a 2.0. He has to report back in Pittsburgh in a week. He's leaving tomorrow."

"Is he going to report?" Jon asked.

"He's not sure. He said he has some family living in Canada, so he might go there, but he really doesn't want to leave the country."

"Better than getting his ass shot over there."

"It's getting worse, and the worse it gets, the more Tony likes it. Sometimes he's just a dumb fuck," Augie said.

"I'm sick of hearing him sing that damn Green Berets song."

"I don't think he has any idea what it would be like over there. I'm not even sure he could really kill someone. He talks all that military bullshit and killing commies, but he's actually kind of a soft-hearted guy under all the bluster. I don't think he could pull the trigger if push came to shove."

Later that afternoon on Broadway, a Scottsbluff County family of six rode slowly into town from their farm twenty miles outside the city limits with all their windows down in their Chevrolet station wagon. It was as if they were visiting a zoo.

They gaped at the college students who clustered on the street corners and were laughing and yelling. Some carried transistor radios that led to some spontaneous dancing spurred by the music of Wilson Pickett, The Supremes, The Capitols, The Temptations, Percy Sledge, Buffalo Springfield, and dozens of others.

> JT — At first, the local "townies" weren't quite sure what to think of all of us "foreigners" who had invaded their town. Some folks never warmed up to us or the idea of having a bunch of sometimes noisy and liberal-leaning, anti-war young people from the big cities back East invading their small, conservative community, especially the ones who smoked pot on the street corners.
>
> There was also consternation among mostly Scottsbluff fathers when their semi-virginal daughters started dating sex-starved guys from the big cities back East.

In early February, a teenage girl was making out with a Scottie in front of Vic's Pizza. Unfortunately for both, the event was witnessed by her father, a beet farmer from Gering, Nebraska, who had come into town in search of his daughter; she had told him she was visiting a sick girlfriend. It was also unfortunate that neither the boy nor girl saw her father's pickup when it pulled up next to them.

Without saying a word, the father yanked his daughter away from the arms of the young man and put her roughly into the front seat. "I told you to stay away from those college boys," the father said.

"Daddy, you're embarrassing me," the daughter protested.

As the pickup drove away, the daughter smiled and waved to the smiling Scottie, who waved back. Later that year, the girl gave birth to twins. She named one of them after her father.

JT — Most of the townies just saw us as either a curiosity or perhaps something that brought economic potential to the community. To most, it was worth the aggravation of having all of us beer-drinking, sometimes loud kids from back East invade their quiet town in a far corner of Nebraska in exchange for the cash flow we helped create for most of the businesses, but particularly for bars, restaurants, gas stations, the bowling alley, carry-outs, and a bakery.

At the same time, most of the students saw Hiram Scott, the college, as a second or even third chance and the town itself as something like a temporary sanctuary.

Everyone seemed to know, especially the guys, that we might be able to postpone the inevitable, but at some point, the war was going to catch up with us either directly, if we were drafted and sent over there and killed, or indirectly if that same thing happened to a friend or family member.

Like me, almost everyone recognized that the turning of the calendar from 1965 to 1966 was a recognition that the new year would bring some significant changes to our lives.

Many of us wondered out loud over pizza and beer where we would be exactly one year from that time. Would some of us transfer to other schools? Flunk out and end up in a rice paddy with our legs blown off? Wrangle some kind of deferment from the Selective Service and be working at a job in California, New York, or Des Moines? Or get a farmer's daughter pregnant and become a permanent resident of a farm in Scottsbluff?

Of our immediate group, the future for one of us seemed like pretty much a sure thing.

The Hiram Scott basketball team played a small college from Iowa and beat them 112 to 63. But the score was not as bad as it could have been. Forddy Anderson's team, led by Jimmy along with nine other former high school All-Americans, had destroyed nearly every team it played, including some big-time programs like the University of Denver, New Mexico, and the University of Montana.

Many of the players had been kicked out of previous schools for various infractions, flunked out, or, in the case of their 6'10" center, had knocked out his former coach for benching him because the player had been late for practice.

Given Forddy's reputation, he was able to meld a group of malcontents into a powerhouse that was getting some national attention. However, Jimmy Davis was clearly the star who would seemingly rise until he made it all the way to the NBA. But it was clear to everyone who watched him play that he had the talent to do more than just make it to the NBA— he had genuine star power on and off the court.

By late February, Jimmy's stats began to get the attention of NBA scouts, and not surprisingly, his little "kerfuffle" back in Philly seemed like a minor infraction and a "boys will be boys" misstep. Especially since he was averaging twenty-nine points and fourteen rebounds a game. It appeared the NBA could be more forgiving than the Villanova coach.

JT — The first time I saw Jimmy play, I couldn't help but notice how black he was. I mean, I knew he was Black, but on the court, maybe because of the lights or sweat, he was the blackest guy I had ever seen. He reminded me of pictures of African men carrying spears while running after game in the savannahs.

Jimmy was also heavily muscled for a guy so slender. Having watched NBA basketball my whole life, I, along with everyone else, knew Jimmy had the "right stuff," and now his dream was getting closer and closer with each college game he played.

After what he told me happened to him back at Villanova, I wanted to see Jimmy become an NBA star. He was a good guy, everyone liked him, and in the end, him leaving Philly and coming to a small town seemed to have opened him up in terms of personality.

After five months on campus, Jimmy appeared to blossom on and off the court. And given he was friendly and soft-spoken, he was a great ambassador for the team in Scottsbluff, where many of the residents had never met or spoken to a Black person, let alone a Black superstar athlete.

While there were a few other Blacks in Scottsbluff, along with several Asians, Native Americans, and Mexicans, those folks were joined by New Yorkers, Philadelphians, New Jerseyites, Chicagoans, and people from just about everywhere else. The small town had become a kind of melting pot where little things like skin color, religion, heritage, and where you came from really didn't matter all that much. All that mattered was how you treated people. Of course, if you could perform a 360-degree dunk from the foul line, that would be nice too.

There was still the ongoing rift between what seemed like the preponderance of white males, particularly veterans of World War II and the Korean War, and the Hiram Scott student body, but the confrontations were now verbal and not physical. I suspected the hot rhetoric had cooled when six more local young men had died in the war over several months.

In early March, about forty students, along with some of the younger professors, gathered at a nice off-campus house that had been rented back in the fall by a group of guys from Philly. As the norm for their famous parties, beer, wine, and food were in abundance. As was also the norm, two attractive women from Washington, DC, sat on a couch on Alan's lap and laughed at his wit and charm.

JT — The big difference between Hiram Scott students and students at other colleges was more than the gaps in SAT scores; it was money. Sure, Harvard and Princeton had students who came from wealthy families, but Hiram Scott kids could, in terms of family net worth, match nearly any school.

While there were many guys like me who came from middle-class families, there were not a lot of poor kids. The reason was that tuition was very high, and the early academic standards at Hiram Scott were very low. If you had the cash and needed a college deferment, good old Hiram Scott College had a seat for you.

But poor grades and low test scores did not always equate to stupidity. It did equate in many cases to laziness, immaturity, large trust funds, and frequently the knowledge there was a job waiting for you in Daddy's business if you could keep from being drafted and sent to the jungles of Vietnam and getting your ass shot.

The party got off to a rousing start when three girls from Milwaukee pantomimed a Supremes song perfectly, which led to some guys spontaneously forming groups to mimic the Four Tops, The Temptations, and The Beach Boys. It became a bit of a back-and-forth contest and included the guys suggesting the losers of the pantomime contest had to strip. The women's objection was not to the rules, but rather that it was too early in the evening for such a performance. The guys were told to be patient.

It appeared each corner of the house had different constituents who always seemed to hang out together no matter where they went. In one corner, near the kitchen door, was the son of a successful Hollywood producer and his friends. That group drank chardonnay and nibbled on cheese and crackers. On the other side of the room were a bunch of overweight guys from New York who drove Continentals and Cadillacs, ate pizza and drank scotch, habits they inherited from their mafia member fathers.

Another group, focused on keeping the music playing, were the sons of two U.S. Senators and two U.S. Congressmen, all four of whom supported the Vietnam War, including increasing the number of boys sent to fight, so long as it wasn't one of *their* boys. That group ate ham sandwiches and chips.

There was also a group of students in the kitchen who were pilots and had flown their own or their family's private plane to Scottsbluff. They ate pot stickers and rice and discussed the latest in aviation radar equipment.

JT — I often wondered why everyone at Hiram Scott seemed to get along so well. Except for Tony and Augie, there were few fights among the students; people were friendly, helpful, liked to party, and seemed to bond.

It could have been that we all felt we were outsiders, and we clung to each other against what began as an unknown environment and population. There was also an element of the rich kids helping the poorer ones like me. Many times, the rich kids bought food and beer for parties. The rich kids would also pick up the tab if a big group of us went out to dinner or a movie together. No one said anything or made a big deal about it—it just happened.

I have also wondered if those kinds of things would have occurred if we had all gone to a big college back East together, or did us being outsiders together create a different kind of relationship or bond among the Scotties?

In a way, the frequent parties we went to were like a substitute for the families and friends we had left behind back home, wherever home was. I think we all needed to be with other people, although I believe most of us realized this was a transient and temporary time of our lives. The uncertainty of the war added to the idea that no one knew where they would be the next year or if we would *be* at all.

Chapter 16

Business Is Business

Alan was one of only twenty students in the Monday morning Western Civilization class, which normally had over ninety attendees. The professor noticed.

"Did everyone catch the flu over the weekend?"

Alan shrugged his shoulders, then took copious notes in three notebooks when the lecture began.

> JT — Alan's "academic consulting" business had grown to the point that he'd go to most classes whether he was enrolled in the class or not, take detailed notes, then sell those notes to those who would prefer to sleep in, rather than attend an 8:15 a.m. class. But Alan discovered that his strategy also worked for classes scheduled all through the day.
>
> He had gotten so busy, he came to me for help, and we met for lunch at Vic's.

"Look, I need some backup for classes I can't attend. I'm already attending seven or eight classes. You're smart. You can go to the classes I can't, and I'll give you a cut."

"I could do the same thing you're doing and keep it all."

"True, but I've perfected a formula and developed a following. Plus, everyone knows my stuff will get them at least a C or they get their money back. Besides, if you and I get into a price war, our prices will go down and we both make less money. Most importantly, it would be fun with you and me working together."

JT — I knew Alan was right, but I wanted to at least try to get a better deal so he would at least respect my vast business acumen. It worked. I got a better percentage cut, and he later said I negotiated like a champ.

We developed a system that included each of us attending as many classes per week as we could fit in without missing our own classes. Alan would collect the cash every Thursday afternoon from our clients; then he and I would meet every Saturday for lunch and have a cash distribution.

Alan and I started working together in preparation for spring midterms. That academic pressure allowed us to raise our prices. After all, with Johnson substantially escalating the war, we developed a very solid marketing slogan reminding our classmates of the cost of poor grades: "Pay us now, and don't die in a rice paddy later."

Over the next few months, Alan and I made some serious cash. In fact, I was able to get new tires on the Ford, buy some new clothes, and even spring for a weekend trip back to San Diego to visit my parents and see Anna. Mainly to see Anna.

I purposely surprised Anna and did not tell her I was coming home for the weekend. When she answered the door, she just stood there for a minute and said nothing, but then tears rolled down her face, and she kissed me.

To point out the obvious, I had kissed girls before, but *that* kiss— that singular and perfect, never-to-be-forgotten kiss—was one that stayed with me even after I had to leave and return to Scottsbluff. Seriously, it was one hell of a kiss.

Without telling Anna, I had applied to Stanford but discovered it would not take any of my credits from Hiram Scott. But since the college deferment was only for four years, I needed to find a college that would take my credits. As soon as I returned to campus, I started that search.

In terms of a search for female companionship, as in for the rest of my life, I figured that search was over. I only hoped Anna felt the same.

Chapter 17

Anna Decided

When she watched Jon drive away on his way to Nebraska, Anna felt a combination of relief and regret. Relief, in that she had finally conjured up the nerve to talk to the guy she had secretly been in love with for years. And regret that after only five minutes, he was gone. And worse, she might never see him again. "This could be a damn Shakespearian tragedy," she said to herself.

Later that night she walked into the family's den while her parents were watching *The Lawrence Welk Show* and proclaimed without fanfare that "I've decided to marry Jon from across the street."

Her mother turned to Anna and asked, "Is Jon aware of his pending marriage?"

"No, but he will be okay with it when he does, although that may take some time."

Without further comment Anna turned and walked out of the room.

Her father, without looking up from a performance from The Lennon Sisters, told his wife, "That poor bastard might as well just say yes now and be done with it."

"I wonder where she gets that attitude?" his wife replied, knowing exactly where Anna got that attitude.

For the rest of her senior year in high school, Anna wrote to Jon every day. Even if she had nothing of real importance to write, she wrote anyway. She wanted to make sure he wouldn't forget her and fall in love with some Cornhusker maiden.

She did date occasionally but made sure the guys knew she was dating someone else and was even kind of engaged, almost, even though that guy she said she was almost engaged to had no fucking idea of his status.

She had been broken-hearted when she learned about Valerie and the impact that situation had on Jon's life. She knew Jon was super smart but that he had just messed up and made a mistake that other guys had made with other "Valeries."

As the weeks, then months, rolled by, Anna looked forward to Sunday nights, when Jon would call her collect and they would talk for as long as her bank account would allow. Her parents said it would be okay if Jon called on "their dime," but Anna said she would pay for the calls since Jon was going to be a smashing success as a writer someday, and he said he would pay her back for all those calls. He did.

When Jon did write, he told her of what was happening at Hiram Scott, and she could tell the war was becoming more and more of an issue for him. Not that he was afraid he would get drafted and sent over to kill folks he had no grudge against, but that the war was beginning to seep into the everyday lives of both students and the citizens of Scottsbluff, and the stress was getting to both groups.

This stress was amplified when young men from the town began to die in Vietnam, and what had been a war thousands of miles away was becoming local. Battle lines were being drawn like in a hundred other cities between pro-war and anti-war factions, not unlike the Civil War stories Anna had read about.

She decided to join in some anti-war marches in and around San Diego and even took a bus to San Francisco to be part of a huge demonstration there. She could tell Jon was pleased when she told him of her involvement.

While in San Francisco, she visited Palo Alto and the Stanford campus. It was everything she hoped it would be, and she gladly joined in another anti-war protest that happened to be taking place on campus during her visit.

After months of missing Jon, sending him a couple of hundred letters and a couple of dozen Sunday night calls, she began to wonder if he really felt the same way she did about him or if perhaps she had on the basis of one brief face-to-face encounter misjudged her own feelings.

When Anna opened her front door over spring break in 1966 and saw Jon standing there with that crooked smile on his face, she intuitively knew that he was the one. No fucking doubt. She had been right about him and her and them. She knew it.

She had grown up seeing Jon from across the street and thought he was a pretty cool guy as early as fifth grade.

She would fantasize about him finally recognizing her and at least saying hello when they were in their respective front yards, but even when she knew he had seen her while he washed his car and she watered her parents' grass, he never even acknowledged her.

During her sophomore year in high school, Anna would see Jon and Valerie walk around school holding hands, and she wanted to run up to him and scream, "She is no good for you, Jon," but knew she could never do anything so overly dramatic, so she kept her mouth shut and hoped something would happen to cause Jon and Valerie to break up, and Jon would come to his senses. Valerie getting pregnant never really entered her mind as a possible breakup scenario.

But then she learned from her sister that maybe Valerie was not pregnant after all and wondered why Jon had still been kicked off the sports teams and lost his appointment to the Naval Academy. It didn't seem fair, and now her affection for Jon, although unrequited at the time, was enhanced by her feeling sorry for him and how he had been treated by Valerie and the school.

Back in high school, she had wanted to approach him for months but always chickened out because she really had no idea what she would say to him. When she heard from her mother that Jon would be leaving for some college in Nebraska on that Saturday morning, she kept looking out her living room window for her chance to say goodbye.

The kiss thing was always in the back of her mind, and when she had stuck her head into the driver's side window a few inches, she had hoped he would be overcome by love and affection and kiss *her*, but she later realized, given the Valerie episode, he was understandably reluctant to act on any impulse of that kind.

Since Jon's actual actions did not match Anna's fantasy, in which he would feel compelled to kiss her goodbye, she instead thought, *What the hell* and decided to kiss him whether he liked it or not. After nearly a minute-long kiss, she concluded he liked it and was reasonably sure he would write to her. She was accurate on both counts.

During her final year of high school, Anna dated some guys, but they were in her mind placeholders for Jon. The weekend he came to visit her was not only a surprise, but this time, it lived up to all the fantasies she had had regarding finally being alone with Jon.

CHAPTER 18

SCOTTSBLUFF SPRING

Even though it was only in the low sixties, a group of Scotties—including Tony, Augie, Jon, Jimmy, Gus, Alan, and three of Alan's favorite female friends—decided it was time to push the season and head out to Lake Alice and soak up some badly needed Vitamin D.

The girls braved the cool weather and at Alan's suggestion wore the sexy bikinis selected and purchased by him. They all agreed Alan had great taste in women's clothing, and the price was right.

A transistor radio blared "Bus Stop" by the Hollies, and everyone sang along. The next song was "Ballad of the Green Berets," and everyone but Tony moaned. Instead, Tony belted out his favorite song and began to march around the beach, now only a few months from being able to enlist and do the real thing and by doing so strike fear in the hearts of the Viet Cong.

"He's really into that military stuff, isn't he?" Jon asked Augie while lying next to him on a beach towel.

"Yeah, ever since he was a kid, he was always playing with toy rifles, dressing up like a soldier, and wanting to shoot as many guys as possible."

"Think your mom will be able to get him to stay in college another year?"

"No way. He's going to enlist the minute he passes his physical. I'm afraid he's going to be over there for a week and get his ass shot. That'll destroy Mom."

"Why's he so gung-ho?"

"I don't know. He's a good kid, but he's hardheaded, and nothing is going to stop him from going over there and fighting."

When the song finally ended, the group applauded Tony's performance. He bowed in response and said, "Hey, let's do some recon. I'm tired of laying around this beach all day."

"Take a rifle and shoot a couple hundred Viet Cong while you're walkin' around the lake. I'll be here when you get back," Gus said.

"I'm stayin' here too. I need to work on my tan," Jimmy said.

Gus looked over at Jimmy, paused for effect, and said, "You're already so black, when you drink water, you piss coffee."

Suddenly, everyone on the beach got quiet, not sure how to react to Gus's attempt at not-so-delicate racial humor. Jimmy slowly took off his sunglasses and glared at Gus. Gus glared back, although he had to look up to do so.

The white 5'6" Gus and the Black 6'8" Jimmy had become close friends over the year, and now everyone was afraid one semi-racist joke was going to mess everything up in terms of the guys' friendship. For months they had hung out together all the time, laughing and teasing each other, but now it appeared Gus was about to get his Greek ass kicked.

"Hey, white boy, you shouldn't go swimming today," Jimmy said.

"Why not, Buckwheat?"

"'Cause crackers get soggy when wet, you fucking albino dwarf."

Gus glared at Jimmy.

Gus had become semi-legendary around school for his impromptu religious ceremony for a 1953 Chrysler New Yorker and seemed like he had finally come out of a shell that he had wrapped himself in when he first came to Scottsbluff. Since he had trouble in the classroom in high school back in Boston and barely graduated, he and his parents knew he had little chance of being accepted anywhere else but Hiram Scott. So, he enrolled in hopes the war would end before his number was called.

His parents were happy to hear he was flourishing at Hiram Scott in the classroom and in making friends. It even appeared he might someday earn a college degree, even though it wasn't from Harvard, where his mother worked in the cafeteria.

"You get any blacker, and your blood type will come back as burnt," Gus declared, as he fought to hold his glare and adding a mean-looking squint in hopes of scaring Jimmy.

The squint did not work. "You know what they call it when a dancin' white boy has a seizure?"

"What?"

"An improvement," Jimmy said.

> JT — Maybe it was because he was so short or maybe he was just so homesick and stayed in the background, but the first few weeks on campus, Gus was kind of invisible. But then he met Jimmy in class one day, and they just hit it off, teasing and giving each other grief all the time.

Gus held his glare but this time even added a raised right eyebrow when he said, "You get any blacker, when you go outside the streetlights will come on."

> JT — In the end everyone seemed to adopt Gus and make him part of the group. I think he liked that. I know he liked that.

"Hey, Gus, do you know what you call a Greek guy with a sheep under his arm?"

"No, James, I don't, but I'm sure you're going to tell me."

"A pimp from Boston."

> JT — At that point, neither guy could take it anymore, and they both broke down in laughter, then high-fived each other. Having seen their act many times before, Tony had a plan.

"Let's go. Those two idiots will do this for an hour."

> JT — As the rest of us walked away from Jimmy and Gus, we could hear them laughing in the distance as they continued their verbal back-and-forth.

"Those guys ought to go on the road as a comedy team," Augie said.

"Yeah, when I get famous for bein' a war hero, I could be their manager and get them on the *Smothers Brothers* TV show," Tony offered.

JT — For the next half hour, under a warming sun, we took a circuitous path that rose and encircled the perimeter of the lake. At the highest point, we could see the outline of buildings in downtown Scottsbluff.

"We used to come out here as kids and hike all over this place before my dad died. I've missed it," Alan said.

"This place is kinda pretty," Augie admitted.

"Yeah, but it ain't like Jersey," Tony helpfully reminded everyone.

"Yeah, it's not noisy, dirty, smelly, and crowded," Augie helpfully reminded Tony.

"Why do you hate Jersey so much, ass face?"

"Are you deaf, fuckhead? I just explained why."

At the top of a hill, the group sat on large rocks and soaked up their share of sunshine. The warmth felt good after months of cold, ice, snow, and darkness. Below them they could see Gus and Jimmy splashing in the lake like little kids.

"I can't believe those morons are swimming in that lake. The water is freezing," Augie said.

"I put my foot in there, and it damn near froze off," Jon said.

"The water will warm up by late June, but you guys will miss that," Alan reminded.

A few minutes later the group could hear Jimmy yelling in the distance.

"Those guys are still at it," Jon said.

Suddenly, the sound coming from Jimmy was not laughter.

"Gus! Gus! Where the hell are you?" Jimmy screamed.

JT — From where we were about a half mile away, all we could see was Jimmy jumping into the lake time after time, then screaming Gus's name when he resurfaced. At first, we thought he was just screwing around. But then we realized we could no longer see Gus.

It took us about fifteen minutes to run back over the rocks and dirt, to the beach. After telling one of the girls to take a car and go for help, the rest of us immediately dove into the frigid water, trying to find Gus.

After searching for twenty minutes, one by one, we all came back to shore as the biting cold water overcame us. Except Jimmy. He kept diving into the water. His once-black skin had turned to a dark purple color, and his breathing had become raspy and shallow.

Three of us finally had to pull him out of the water when it appeared he would drown too or die from exposure.

Later, our group all stood around Jimmy, wrapped in blankets the rescue squad had given us after they finally arrived.

"I told him not to go back into the water. It was too cold. But he wouldn't listen," Jimmy said softly.

"It's not your fault, Jimmy. You did everything you could," Jon said.

"Why wouldn't he listen to me, Jon?"

JT — They didn't find Gus for two more days. One of the rescue guys said Jimmy was lucky he hadn't drowned too as his core body temperature had fallen below ninety degrees, and he was close to severe hypothermia, which can cause people to go into shock or even have heart attacks. Had either one occurred, Jimmy would have also died.

Later the cops told us we couldn't see Gus because his body was bloated, all black and blue, and did not look like him. He had also been all torn up by the grappling hooks they had used to finally locate him in twenty feet of frigid water. We were not sure who called Gus's parents in Boston and told them the news.

Later that night, Jon sat on the steps of the Lincoln Hotel and wrote in his journal.

JT — It dawned on me how little we actually knew about Gus. What we did know was we all liked him. But that was how most of our relationships were back then. We had fun and cared for each other, but in the end, we never really learned a lot about anyone.

We all seemed to understand that our relationships were transitory, mainly because we knew most of us would never see each other again. Therefore, the need or even desire to learn someone's innermost secrets was not important.

What I did learn from most of the people I met at Hiram Scott was we all had some baggage that we were lugging around, whether it was getting a girlfriend pregnant, mooning a coach's wife, caring for a terminally ill mother, or being petty crooks in the greatest fucking state in the union.

But Gus dying changed things. Over the first seven months in Scottsbluff, it was a time for many of us to escape or even heal from the things that made us come there in the first place.

Most of us, it seemed, didn't select Hiram Scott as the place we wanted to come for a stellar higher education. Rather, events brought us there for a myriad of varied reasons. Reasons that were, in some cases, never discussed. Because of that, we all seemed to understand each other, accept each other, and were careful not to probe too deeply for fear of learning more than we wanted to learn. Or discover more than someone wanted to share.

I guess Gus's death was like a wake-up call for all of us. The first several months of college had been a lot of fun and games. But it felt like things had changed.

The irony of Gus was that he had wanted to enlist in the army, but his parents would not let him. They were afraid he would go to Vietnam and get killed. As a result, the war in Vietnam had indirectly sent him to a lake in Nebraska, where he had been killed. It seemed the plan for Gus was to get killed somewhere, somehow, no matter what he did.

In late May, Jon and Alan walked back from a movie at the Midwest Theater following Tony and Augie, who were arguing yet again, before getting into a shoving match on the street.

"It's a wonder one of those guys hasn't put the other into intensive care yet," Jon said.

"Probably just a matter of time."

"I think you're right."

"Have you decided what you're doing next year yet?" Alan asked.

"I have a good shot to get accepted at Northwestern. Doesn't look like they will take all my credits from here, but I can make those classes up in the summer and take some extra hours next winter. How about you?"

"When Mom passes, I'll reapply to Yale and see what happens. I'll probably stay here next year either way, but if you were going to come back, I thought we could room together."

"I'd do that, but Northwestern has great journalism and writing programs, and I hope I can sneak in there. Maybe you can come up to Chicago for a couple weekends and we can do Rush Street."

"That would be fun. What do you want to do when you graduate?"

"I want to write, but I'm not sure if that means journalism, creative writing, or even writing screenplays. Guess I want to do it all."

"Then do it all."

"What do you want to do, besides rule the world?"

"I want to get a business degree, then my MBA. Maybe start my own business. I see myself living in New York City and spending time on Wall Street. That would be exciting."

"We have to make sure we stay in touch after this year."

"Hell, yes, we should. We should also have a party before we all scatter. A real blowout. A puke-your-guts-out type ridiculous gala."

Two weeks later, a sign in front of a large two-story house just outside downtown Scottsbluff said, FINALS OVER PARTY! (Bring beer, pizza, and weed.)

Given the warmer temperatures the students drove their cool car collection and parked them in the front yard of the house. A gullwing Mercedes, a Porsche 356, a 427 Corvette convertible, and assorted Cadillacs, Continentals, and T-Birds were among the thirty cars that sat under two large oak trees.

From inside the house, "Devil with the Blue Dress" by Mitch Ryder and The Detroit Wheels had the crowd dancing, singing, and drinking, and it wasn't even eight o'clock yet.

The house was filled with over eighty students. There was an abundance of food, grass, hard liquor, and partially clad women, many of whom did not even attend Hiram Scott but were welcomed with literal open arms by the male students.

Alan and Jon stood in a corner of the living room and looked over the drinking and dancing and smiled at some of the performances, including Tony doing the Gator in front of a beer keg.

"Well, you wanted to see one last puke fest. Looks like you got your wish," Jon said.

"All in the planning, my friend. Also, I have a little surprise for later."

"Like what?"

"You have to wait, but it's something that needs to be done."

"Did you buy another car to drive off a bluff?"

"Be patient, my California friend."

After Alan walked away to tend to three girls seeking his immediate attention, Jon saw Jimmy sitting alone on some stairs near the dining room. "Hey, man, I haven't seen you around the last few days … How you doin'?" Jon asked.

"You know me, aways hittin' the books."

"How are you holding up?"

"Okay."

"Really?"

"I met Gus's parents when they came in from Boston to pick up the body," Jimmy said softly.

"That must have been tough."

"Funny thing was, he'd told them he had a new friend out here named Jimmy and we were thinkin' of forming a comedy team and going on the road and becoming the next Martin and Lewis."

"Was he serious?"

"I don't know. We'd get together and kick around crazy stuff like that. You know, just some crazy bullshit. But the funny thing is, he never told his parents I was Black. All he told them was I was the best friend he ever had. I thought that was pretty cool." Jimmy's voice had become a whisper.

"He was a cool guy, and I guess he never told them because he didn't give a damn what color you were. You were his best friend and that was that."

Jimmy turned to Jon and said, "Yeah, man, that's how I saw it too."

"What did his parents say when they met you?"

"His mom wouldn't shake my hand and just kinda glared at me. Then she just turned and walked away when I tried to talk to her. His dad came up to me, got right up on my face, and called me a fucking nigger coward who let his son drown." As he spoke, Jimmy downed several swigs of scotch, as tears formed in his eyes.

Jon reached out and put his arm on Jimmy's shoulder. "Fuck those assholes, Jimmy. Someone should tell them how you nearly drowned yourself trying to save Gus. You know the truth, all of us who were there know the truth, but most importantly, Gus knows the truth."

Jimmy nodded and looked at Jon. "Yeah, Gussie knows."

> JT — Over the next several hours, the party maintained its momentum. It seemed obvious no one wanted to leave Alan's puke fest until absolutely necessary, meaning all the beer was gone, or the cops came.

While "What Becomes of the Brokenhearted" by Jimmy Ruffin played in the background, couples danced and made out on anything they could find, including the floor. A haze of pot had created a yellow, mellow mist in the house that allowed even non-smokers to get a serious buzz.

On a corner couch, Jimmy, Jon, Augie, and Tony sat shoulder to shoulder, either too drunk or too tired to move. A few minutes later, Alan entered the room and proceeded to turn down the music.

"Okay, guys, I need to say something before you all pass out on your asses."

Assuming that Alan was about to say something profound and maybe even sentimental about all of us saying goodbye in a few hours, the crowd actually paid attention to him when he brought a chair from the kitchen and stood on it in the middle of the room.

"Since school started last fall, there have been some ridiculous rumors floating around about me that I want to clear up before everyone heads home this weekend. First of all, I did NOT make a million dollars getting most of your collective asses through school this year, but it was close."

The students raised their glasses and shouted, "Yay, Alan!"

"I also heard I was running a bookie operation in my spare time and … okay, that was actually true, but no one should be going around town talking about those things."

Tony looked at Augie and asked, "Did you know that little fucker was a bookie?"

"Nope, cuz he doesn't dress like one," Augie related from experience.

Alan continued, "But the most ridiculous thing I have heard this year from many of you regarded my … male organ."

"It's called a dick, you dick," Tony reminded Alan.

"Okay, it's called a dick. Ladies, please forgive that unfortunate colloquial use of a noun. It is regrettable that so many of you believed what you heard and further made the assumptions that these beautiful and virginal young women—at least they were virginal back in October—standing here next to me now had followed me around campus because of a preposterous rumor that I had a ten-inch …"

"It's called a dick, you dick," Tony reminded again.

"Very well, a dick it shall henceforth be called. Once and for all to prove this unfair, scandalous, and ridiculous rumor is indeed false, I am forced, despite my well-known modesty, to prove beyond any doubt whatsoever and reveal the truth, here tonight, right in front of your very own eyes."

Alan balanced on the kitchen chair and began to slowly unzip his pants. As he did, someone turned on Marvin Gaye's "How Sweet It Is to Be Loved by You," while the crowd became silent as if they were about to witness a solar eclipse or a two-headed calf being born or, as rumor had it, a real live ten-inch dick, obviously the latter being the rarest of all.

But then he stopped in mid-unzip. "Obviously, that kind of scurrilous rumor is unfair to these young ladies and their families because it makes it appear they'd simply kept the pleasure of my company as a source for their sexual gratification and for my *lasciviousness.* Look it up, Tony."

The crowd cheered.

JT — It was at this point that all of us sitting near Alan got the joke since we saw something moving in Alan's underwear that appeared to wrap halfway around his skinny waist. It also appeared to be alive.

The crowd was no longer cheering—instead, it was eerily quiet while everyone stared at Alan's undulating crotch.

Alan resumed his unzipping and said, "What is truly unfair to me, and my lady friends, is that all you guys really think these women could be seduced by a ten-inch …"

"It's called a dick," the crowd yelled.

In silence and as a unit, the crowd edged closer to Alan. When he finally dropped his Jockey white underwear, something fell out and bounced between his legs, right above his right knee. Several gasps could be heard in the crowd.

"See, it's not ten inches … it's eleven inches!"

JT — The crowd in the house went fucking nuts. There was cheering, laughing, and pointing as Alan did a 360-degree turn on the chair with that thing he now called a dick spinning out into space.

It looked unreal and awe-inspiring at the same time. Almost a religious experience. Several girls left their dates just to get a closer look at "The Thing" as it was to be forever known in the annals of Hiram Scott College history.

The women who had been surrounding Alan all year were suddenly looked at with a great deal more respect. After all, it took courage to date Alan. And required the assistance of some friends who could share the burden.

The crowd cheered Alan, who took several bows, and then clapped toward his faithful female followers.

Alan's performance was the perfect capper to a perfect party. While there was indeed some puke, it was kept at a reasonable level; there had been great music, far more than enough booze, some food, although I can't recall what kind, no fights, and probably no more than three to four future pregnancies. A great way to end the school year.

CHAPTER 19

GOODBYES ARE A BITCH

Just before the sun rose, Alan, Jon, Augie, Jimmy, and Tony trudged back toward the dorm. The puke fest had finally worn them out. In the eastern sky, the pending daybreak had created an orange-pink aura just above the horizon with purple hues that spread out over the prairie.

As he looked up at nature's handiwork, Jon said, "They sure do have beautiful sunrises out here."

When the five of them stopped to look eastward and take in the beauty of "a serene, almost magical moment" as Jon called it, Tony best captured the innermost thoughts of what all of them were thinking when he said, "Yeah, cool, let's go get some fucking donuts."

"The bakery doesn't open for another thirty minutes," Alan noted.

"Fuck it, we'll wait," Augie said, speaking for the group.

The five guys sat down on the curb in front of the bakery and waited for the sunrise and warm donuts. To pass the time, Tony had lifted a morning paper that had been delivered minutes earlier to the front door of the unopened drugstore.

"Jon, what time do you leave today?" Alan asked.

"I'm gonna get a few hours' sleep and head out this afternoon."

"Jimmy?"

"I'm takin' the ten o'clock bus. Bet I'll sleep all the way to Philly."

"How about you guys," Jon asked Tony and Augie.

"We got an afternoon flight back later today," Augie said.

"Fuck yeah, can't wait to get home to Jersey, great fucking state."

After several minutes of silence, Tony made an announcement. "Listen to this. General Westmoreland, a great fucking guy by the way, says, *I see no course of action open to us except to reinforce our efforts in South Vietnam with additional U.S. or third-party troops as rapidly as possible.*"

"Gee, that's great news," Jon said, his sarcasm escaping Tony.

"Fuckin A, that means I didn't miss the war after all."

"I have a feeling there's going to be plenty of war left for you and a few hundred thousand other guys, Tony," Jon noted.

After more silence, Alan asked, "Do you guys think any of us will ever see each other again?"

"Fuck yeah, we'll get together. You can book that," Tony guaranteed.

"Sure we will," Augie agreed.

"Of course," Jon said, although with less assurance.

"Then we should make a plan," Jimmy said.

"What kind of plan?" Alan asked.

"You know, to get together sometime like next year or the year after, like a reunion just for us guys," Jimmy answered.

JT — Sitting on that curb, as the sun rose, we all knew the reality was we'd never see each other again. After all, we were all heading to different places, to do different things with different people.

There would be new friends, marriages, kids, mortgages, successes, and failures. Maybe even sicknesses or death. As we sat there waiting for the warm donuts in the early morning, we all knew the idea of getting together again was total bullshit. Maybe that was why I said what I said.

"I got an idea. Let's all promise to meet back here in fifty years; June 8th, 2016, at six in the morning, we'll get donuts."

"Are you fuckin' nuts? We'll all be dead by then," Tony said optimistically.

"Well, you will be if you go to Vietnam," Augie said.

"That's a cool idea, Jon. I'll show up. Let's see, fifty years from now we'll all be, oh God, we'll all be old as hell," Alan said after doing some quick math.

"Who the hell wants to live to be that old?" Augie asked, expanding on his family's innate optimism.

"We'll probably be all old and wrinkled in fifty years, and even Alan's dick won't work, and I gotta say that is one impressive hog you got there, Alan, but I'll show up if everybody else promises to," Tony said.

"Thanks, Tony, that comment about my unit means a lot coming from you since we all know Jersey is a place where a lot of big dicks live."

"I won't miss it for nothin'," Jimmy promised.

"Me either, but I wonder what it will be like then, what we will be like," Augie said.

> JT — For the next twenty minutes, we sat on the curb in Scottsbluff, Nebraska, and shared our predictions and plans for the next fifty years.

"No shit, I'm going to be a fucking war hero. I mean it. I'm gonna kill a bunch of commies and set a world's record. That'll get me a bunch of medals, and then I'm going to open a judo studio after I learn judo in the army or marines, or just become a movie star. I might get married, but probably not. Need to give all the ladies a chance."

"Great fucking plan, you idiot," Augie said.

"At least I got a plan, shit for brains."

"I do too! After I graduate from college, I've decided to join the Peace Corps. I heard it's hard, but you get to see the world and help people. Besides, I could never really shoot anyone. Plus, I have to try and undo some of what my crazy brother will be doing in Nam."

Tony slugged Augie in the arm because … well, just because.

"How about you, Alan?" Jon asked.

"When Mom passes, I want to go to Harvard or Yale and get my MBA. Go to work on Wall Street and make a million bucks before I'm thirty. Then I'm going to move to Europe and live in a Swiss chalet and drive my Porsche through the Alps with my Swiss actress/model wife."

"Hell, if I was you, Alan, with the equipment you got, I'd go straight into the porn business and make a million bucks that way. That would be a lot more fun. Then move to Cherry Hill. That's in Jersey," Tony said.

The guys laughed at Tony's suggestion, even though it sounded reasonable on many levels.

"Jon?" Alan asked.

"After I get out of Northwestern, I want to write books or maybe work for the *Chicago Tribune* as a feature writer. It would also be cool to write movie scripts in Hollywood. Don't think I'll get married till I'm forty, but when I do, I want to have maybe five kids."

"God, forty sounds so old," Augie said. The rest of the guys nodded in agreement.

"Maybe Jon can write a story about me, you know, me bein' a war hero when I kill all those commies and get a shit load of medals. Hell, maybe they'll make a movie about me someday," Tony said in a semi-whisper.

"Sounds good to me, but not sure all those dead commies will like the plot," Jon said.

"Fuck them, they're just commies."

Suddenly, the front door to the bakery opened, and the owner stuck a red brick on the sidewalk to keep the door open.

"Morning, boys, you're all here pretty early, but c'mon in. The donuts are cooling on the rack."

JT — We bought a dozen donuts that morning and had our usual two each. The two extras in the bag we saved for and dedicated to Gus. We decided to leave them for him in a spot only Jimmy could reach.

We walked through town to the city park, the spot where I had seen the guys from Chicago administer their public service breast exams that first day on campus. That seemed like a lifetime ago. To Gus, it was.

When we reached the gazebo, Jimmy moved to a nearby oak tree, stretched out his long arm, and stuffed the white bag with two donuts into a small hole in the tree eight feet above the ground.

"Hey, Gussie, we all miss you, little man. Your folks told me what you said about me bein' your best friend and all. I feel the same way. We made a good team, you and me. You know, me bein' tall, real dark, and handsome, and you bein' … you. Just kiddin', man. Things ain't so funny now like they used to be without you bein' around. Hope you're okay, man. Sorry I couldn't …"

JT — Jimmy started to break down, and all of us gathered around him and patted him on the back, trying our best to comfort him when we knew that would be impossible. Even Tony had tears in his eyes, although he tried to hide it, because commie-killing marines are not supposed to cry.

After we left the park, we walked slowly back to the dorm, but no one said a word. Not a single word. It was as if we had said and done everything we could have and should have said and done.

After some perfunctory goodbyes later that morning, we all went our separate ways in an almost nonchalant way, as if we were embarrassed to say serious goodbyes to each other, for those goodbyes would be forever.

Maybe because we were guys, I think all of us were afraid to admit that over one school year, we had helped each other through some tough times. Sure, we laughed our asses off, drank gallons of beer, ate hundreds of pizzas, and did what most college kids do, but we had also lost a mutual friend, we had come to grips with our own weaknesses, and despite everything, we learned more about each other than we thought.

But most importantly, we learned things about ourselves. And for that one year at least, we felt that crazy war had been unable to find us, although we would eventually discover that directly or indirectly, that damn war found nearly everyone in the country one way or another.

Chapter 20

Colorado Springs

It had been Jon's intention to get up around noon on Saturday, the morning after the puke fest, say a final goodbye to Tony and Augie, and then hit the road back to San Diego.

However, the previous night of unlimited beers, some rum, a thick orange vodka concoction, some sloe gin, assorted shots of unknown but potent ingredients, followed by some pizza, meatballs, and potato chips, all washed down by two glazed donuts had taken a toll on his digestive system. In other words, after returning to the dorm and as ordained by the goal of the previous night's festivities, Jon puked his guts out for several hours.

When he finally woke up on Saturday, it was nearly 5 p.m. and his room was unusually quiet, which meant Tony and Augie were not there. What was there, in addition to a crashing headache and a threat of more projectile vomiting in his future, was a note from Augie that was taped to his bathroom mirror.

> *Yo, Jonny, you've been a great roommate, man, thanks for the good times. Me and Tony think you are a pretty cool guy and hope you have a good summer and get into Northwestern. We may come out to Chi-Town sometime and you can show us around. We want to go to Wrigley Field. We were going to wake you and say goodbye, but I heard you gagging your ass off last night so figured you needed to sleep in. Let's get together sometime way before fifty years. Tony says goodbye and will dedicate his first ten dead commies to you. Stay cool, man.*

His first reaction to reading Augie's note was to run into their room and see if they had really left. Then he remembered they had a morning flight out of Scottsbluff and were probably already back in New Jersey by then, which everyone knew was the greatest fucking state in the country.

For some reason, the quiet in the room was eerie and a little depressing to Jon. Two guys he had spent almost every waking hour with over the previous eight months were gone, and it was possible, if not likely, he would never see them again.

He knew Jimmy had left even earlier in the day on a bus bound for Philly, and Alan had said he and his mother were going to visit some relatives in Casper for the weekend. After having a cup of instant coffee, he went downstairs and walked around the empty lobby for a while and thought back to that first day of school. It seemed like yesterday, but so much had happened in such a short period of time.

The chaos of the last few days of school, with studying for finals, parties, and preparing to leave, was now over, and what was left was the quiet and a repeating playback of memories, even though in some cases those memories were only hours old. In the last week none of the guys had really given any thought to the goodbyes that were imminent or more importantly to the people they would never see again.

After heading back up to his room, Jon thought about packing up everything, loading up the Ford, and heading to San Diego right then, but he was still not feeling so great, so he decided to go to bed early and try again the next morning when his head and stomach felt better, if that were possible. Since the puke fest was Alan's idea, he was hoping he at least had a headache up in Casper, but knowing Alan as he did, he figured Alan had found the cure for hangovers.

On Sunday morning Jon rolled out of bed around seven, after ten hours of sleep, and did not feel awful. In fact, he felt pretty damn good and decided to risk another digestive catastrophe and have a goodbye breakfast at the Eagle Café. After a super-hot shower and shave, he packed up his two suitcases and duffle bag and loaded them into the Ford. He decided to keep his room key as a memento and risk the $5.00 fine.

When he pulled up in front of the place that had fed him at least 75 percent of his meals over the previous eight months, he was surprised there was actually an empty spot.

When he entered, he noticed that for the first time since school had started, the café was nearly empty. There were some older guys at the counter, sipping their coffee and reading the *Star-Herald*, and a few of the tables and booths were occupied, but the usual crowd and noise were missing. Jon could not decide if he liked the quieter atmosphere or not.

He ordered some of his favorites, French toast and bacon. After the first bite he figured he was over his stomach ailment and chowed down but then, throwing all caution to the winds, ordered a side of scrambled eggs and hash browns.

In the booth behind him, two college-age guys were having their breakfast, although they did not look familiar. He could overhear their conversation and discovered they had come from Wisconsin on their way to Colorado Springs and the Air Force Academy.

He heard they had driven into town the night before and ran into some mechanical difficulties with their Dodge pickup, in that it threw a rod just before they entered Scottsbluff and then for good measure caught fire. The guys were able to save their stuff from the back of the pickup before the gas tank blew up and the Dodge burned down to the wheels.

The young men spent the previous night at a motel in town and discovered no flights were available into Colorado Springs the next morning. They were given more unwelcome news when they learned the bus they needed to get them to Denver, then on to Colorado Springs, was running behind schedule and would not deliver them to the academy until late that evening, which meant that would be more than six hours after they were supposed to report. Not a good start to their military careers.

Realizing he was not in a real rush to head back to San Diego since Anna would not be there for a week, Jon turned around and posed a suggestion. "Hey, guys, sorry, I wasn't eavesdropping, but I heard what happened last night. I'm heading down to San Diego in a few minutes and can go through Colorado Springs and get you there late this afternoon, if you're interested. It's only about 275 miles. By the way, my name is Jon."

The two young men looked at each other and smiled. Greg, a tall, athletic-looking blond straight out of a Norwegian ski movie, said, "Wow, that would be a life saver. We'd be happy to pay for the gas down there."

His buddy, Patrick O'Hara, a shorter, red-haired, thick-bodied eighteen-year-old, said, "You are a life saver, Jon."

"No problem and no need for gas money; like I said, I was headed in that general direction anyway."

After stuffing the guys' suitcases and bags into every available nook and cranny of Jon's Ford, the three guys headed south from Scottsbluff.

After some small talk Jon asked, "Did I hear you guys were from Wisconsin?"

"We're both from La Crosse. Our families have known each other since before we were born. In fact, our dads served together in World War II," Patrick said.

"Yeah, we live across the street from each other now and played on the same junior league hockey team, went to the same church and school," Greg added.

"We also decided we wanted to fly jets when we were about eight years old, so we applied to the Air Force Academy last year. I knew Greg would get an appointment because he's a freaking genius, but I was kind of surprised I got in."

"Don't listen to him. Patrick is a math savant and a pretty damn good hockey goalie. How about you, Jon—are you in college?" Greg asked.

"Just finished my first year at a small college back in Scottsbluff, called Hiram Scott."

"Don't think I heard of that school," Patrick said.

"Doubt you would have. It's a new school that just opened its doors last fall. Looks like I'll be heading to Northwestern next fall."

"You didn't like it in Scottsbluff?" Patrick asked.

"Actually, I came here because … well, because of some personal issues back in San Diego and needed to get in school quick or risk getting drafted, so I came here for a year."

"Yeah, getting drafted is not a great option," Patrick agreed.

"What will you study at Northwestern?" Greg asked.

"Writing."

"What kind of writing?"

"I want to write it all. Novels, screenplays, short stories, maybe even have my own newspaper column one day."

"I was never very good at writing. Guess I'm not very creative," Greg admitted.

Pat added, "Me either, but I like to read, though. Maybe I'll read your stuff someday. What kind of subjects do you want to write about?"

"Guess that depends on what is happening in the world at the time. You know, the current events."

For several minutes no one followed up with what Jon perceived as a logical next question. So, after five miles, he preempted a response. "You know, I would write about the most important story in the news at the time, like Vietnam is the most important story in the country now."

Again, there was silence from Patrick, who sat in the front seat, and Greg, who sat in the back along with some suitcases and duffle bags.

> JT — I remember wondering at the time if the guys remained quiet when the subject of the war came up because, number one they were polite and did not want to get into what could evolve into a volatile debate on the war with someone they did not know for fear of losing their ride and getting everyone in the Ford pissed off. But I also wondered what my position on the war was at that moment. For eight months most of the people I had been around were anti-war, except for Tony. Yet, he and Augie seemed to represent the extreme polarities of the opinions on the war, and it seemed many American citizens were beginning to take one side of the argument or the other.

After several more minutes, Greg said, "Not sure how you feel about the war, but everyone in both our families back in Wisconsin are dead set against it."

"That's surprising. I would've thought that given your dads' military backgrounds, they would be all for it."

"Maybe it's because they have seen war up close and personal that they are against it. Our dads told us that they lost lots of friends during the war, and many more guys were just messed up psychologically when they came home. But my dad also said that even if the politicians are wrong, the military has a duty to execute its responsibility," Patrick said.

Greg added, "Our dads flew B-17s and B-29s back in World War II and still have nightmares about the innocent people they killed during the bombing raids over Tokyo. I'll bet the guys in Nam now who are doing those strafing runs in Cambodia and North Vietnam feel the same way. You can hate what you're doing but be duty-bound to do what you are ordered to do."

"The pilots could always refuse to do what they're ordered to do," Jon said.

"I guess that is the obvious alternative, but the military would fall apart if a soldier had the option to obey one order, then follow the next order at his discretion," Greg responded.

Patrick said, "I've heard of some guys over there purposely missing their targets if they felt they might bomb a village, hospital, or anything that could kill a bunch of innocents, but their superiors or fellow pilots would soon catch on to that kind of thing, and that pilot would be replaced."

"What do you think about the war, Jon? What would you write about it?" Greg asked.

JT — I wasn't sure how to respond to Greg's question, because he and Patrick seemed like good guys, and I really didn't want to have 250 more miles of argument, but I figured what the hell.

"When you really think about it, nearly all wars are idiotic. They are fundamentally stupid in that millions die, mostly innocent citizens, billions of dollars are wasted, and that colors my opinion about this particular war. I don't think the U.S. is in any danger from North Vietnam or there is a direct long-term threat to our country. We are not protecting a NATO ally, yet we appear to be tying the hands of our military by restricting operations. From what I've read, we could invade Hanoi and overthrow that regime in a month, but we don't. Instead, we bomb and kill innocent villagers and send our own guys—guys like you two—into harm's way. It makes no fucking sense to me. If we stay in this war, we could end up having have ten thousand guys dead over there."

Again, there was silence in the Ford for several miles before Greg said, "I did not decide to go to the Air Force Academy because I wanted to kill poor people living in a nineteenth-century country. In fact, I have sleepless nights wondering how I'll respond to a direct order to do just that. I decided to go to the academy when I was a kid because I wanted to learn to fly. I realized going to fight in a war was always a possibility, but I assumed any war would be like World War II, where we would all want to fight and defend our country and I would do my part."

"Same with me, and our dads understand how different this war is compared to World War II. I guess after Pearl Harbor guys couldn't enlist fast enough. Our country had been attacked, and guys like our dads did their duty. No one likes the idea of war, but some wars *have* to be fought or guys like Hitler or Stalin won't stop until they have strangleholds on the entire world; then they would try to kill each other for total control."

"Okay," Jon said, "I concede a guy like Hitler has to be stopped, but how about Korea, where I read over 36,000 U.S. soldiers were killed? For what? A fucking armistice? Even in World War I there were over 116,000 U.S. deaths if you include all the guys who died in Europe from influenza. If not for that war, those guys would not have died."

"That's not exactly true. Some of those guys would have died of the flu even if they never left home. But I do get your point. No one is saying war solves anything, but the fact is they usually do. Even in Korea, that war stopped the spread of communism at the 38th Parallel, and that armistice is still holding," Greg pointed out.

"And World War II stopped Hitler, and God knows how many more Jews would have died if he had not been stopped. Don't you see that, Jon?"

"Of course I do, but ..."

> JT — For the next two hours, Greg, Patrick, and I debated the relative value and necessity of war. We debated the Kennedy assassination and how things would have been different had Kennedy lived. We debated if the world would survive a nuclear WWIII. We debated who was the best player, Ruth, Cobb, or Williams. Since Ted and I were from San Diego, he got my vote, but I could understand the Cobb vote as well. In fact, for the first time in a year, I was engaging with young men who

I realized were the kind of guys I would have met at Annapolis. It was not that the guys at Hiram Scott were stupid, because they weren't; in fact, in many cases they were incredibly bright and articulate. It was just that guys going for bachelor degrees of science at one of the academies or MIT or an Ivy League school looked at the world through a different lens. Things seemed more black or white to them. As if all life's problems could be solved within the confines of a mathematical equation. That had been me in high school. What I learned from Augie, Tony, Alan, and Jimmy and a lot of the other people in Scottsbluff, including the Walkers, was the world, and the war, was not black and white. It was a series of grays.

When I dropped the guys off at the Air Force Academy later that day, I admit I was a bit jealous. I even considered applying there when I got back home but realized that was a pipe dream and concluded Northwestern was where I needed to go. But I also realized I had learned things in Scottsbluff that would stay with me the rest of my life.

Before the guys said goodbye, we exchanged addresses and phone numbers and vowed to stay I touch. We did.

On my drive from Colorado Springs to San Diego, I had plenty of time to think back over the last year and realized how much my life had changed. How I had changed as a person. How the direction of my career had changed. Even how the world had changed. It seemed to me that meeting Patrick and Greg was a fitting bookend to that year, given they represented a different point of view as to what was happening in the world and what would happen over the next decade.

Scottsbluff and Hiram Scott were now literally and figuratively in my rearview mirror, but the non-classroom education I received there had given me a perspective on things and people I would not have gotten had I gone directly to the Naval Academy. I am not saying it was a better education, but it was definitely a *different* education and one that shaped me more than I knew at the time.

What I did know was Anna would be coming home from a family vacation in less than a week, and at that time, that seemed like such a long time to wait for her. What I didn't know, as I drove into the glare of a setting sun, was how quickly fifty years would pass.

CHAPTER 21

ANNA KNEW STUFF

In May of 2015, at a Lake Forest, Illinois, cemetery, over one hundred mourners gave their condolences to a tall, slender man in a dark blue suit with salt-and-pepper hair. "We're so sorry, Jon" was repeated a hundred times.

Three hours after the ceremony, he returned after everyone had left and talked to Anna's gravesite. He had more to say. He wasn't sure she was listening, but after having talked to her almost every day of their forty-five-year marriage, having no more conversations with her was going to be a tough habit to break and one he was not ready to begin just yet.

Eight months later, Jon stood in the kitchen, sipped his morning tea, and stared out the window into a snow-covered garden and backyard.

> JT — After Anna died, I began to realize the house had too many memories, but I felt guilty selling a place she had loved so much, even though I was sick of the cold weather.
>
> Every time I looked outside, I could see her working in her garden wearing a Cubs hat and trying without much success to sing a Barbra Streisand song. Or an Aretha song or any song for that matter because, truth be told, Anna couldn't carry a tune in a bucket. But what she lacked in voice control and range, she made up in volume and enthusiasm.
>
> When I envisioned her out there singing away, I couldn't keep a smile off my face, but that would soon turn into a recurring and lingering depression based on missing my best friend.

Four months later, Jon once again stood in front of Anna's grave. "Hey, sweet thing, as you may have noticed, I miss the hell out of you. Now

I'm sorry I didn't get some advice from you when I could have so you could tell me what the hell I am supposed to do now. You know how you always liked giving me advice."

JT — It had been almost a year since Anna had died, and I finally told myself to snap the hell out of it and do something creative or labor intensive or even stupid but do something.

The best I could come up with was to clean out the attic, which I had not been up in for at least thirty years. I realized it wasn't something that was going to change my life, but it was something Anna had nagged me for years to get done. I didn't, so I felt an obligation to get up there and clean out that crap, in the hopes that if she was watching, she would say, "Finally."

Over several years, Anna threatened she would put Clorox in my tea or deprive me of sexual pleasure, which I doubted on a number of levels, although I often smelled my tea before I drank it, if I didn't clean out the attic, so I figured if there was a heaven and there was sex in heaven, I better climb the stairs and get to work.

The fact was the idea of rummaging through decades of accumulated stuff that I would have no idea what to do with was precisely why I chose that task. Sort of a penance to Anna for ignoring her "requests" for all those years.

Since I hadn't been up there for decades, I figured it was time.

When Jon climbed up the pull-down ladder and onto the attic floor, he was immediately struck by an aroma of "old." As his eyes adjusted to a dim overhead light, he saw assorted old furniture that he remembered from the '60s, '70s, and '80s and immediately thought, *Goodwill.*

Then he looked at the furniture more closely and began to remember when Anna and he had purchased it, how they had counted every dime and promised not to eat out for a year to finance that table or chair. It also dawned on him why she had been reluctant to sell or give away that old stuff: memories. Anna was big on memories.

For the next twenty minutes, Jon soaked in those same memories one last time but also realized on a certain level, he had been correct. Other folks could still use all this stuff, so he decided Goodwill or some other charity could benefit from Anna's excellent taste in mid-century furniture.

JT — After making my decision on the furniture, I felt that I had finally "done something" as opposed to sitting around the house all day staring at the walls or feeding the squirrels in the backyard. I felt Anna would be proud of me even if I was giving away the solid oak table and chairs she loved so much.

As I was about to head back downstairs, I noticed a stack of what looked like old letters stacked neatly on a shelf. My name was on a piece of paper in a bold Magic Marker that had been tacked to a ceiling beam. I realized what I was looking at were letters we had written to each other while I was in Scottsbluff.

The stack of letters was about twelve inches high and tied in pink ribbon. I sat on the floor, untied the ribbon, and discovered the letters were in order date-wise from when they were written; they were letters we had sent to each other when we were apart all those years ago.

I recalled I had saved the letters she had sent me, and when I returned home, I gave them to her, and she, unbeknownst to me, had saved each one for all these years.

The sad fact was I had written to her maybe once a week. She had written to me every day. Every damn day. As I sat there, I felt guilty as hell about that and said, "Sorry, Anna, I should have written more often."

When I opened one letter after the other and read what she was doing in high school that week, or what I was doing at Hiram Scott, I began to smell the fragrance of Ambush perfume and remembered her telling me she sprayed each letter with that perfume because she thought I would like it. I did, I liked it a lot, and now the half-century-old fragrance triggered my brain and made me smile and tear up at the same time. It was painful. It was cathartic. It was joyful.

The last letter in the pile was different. It was in a bright red envelope and was dated just after we had learned of Anna's prognosis. I saw my name written on the outside. My hands began to shake as I opened the letter.

Hi, Jonny,

I knew you would eventually get up here, so I decided to make sure you saw our old letters to remind you how much I loved your butt, and it sounded like you felt the same. We were young and in love, and we were lucky to have that in our lives, the rest of our lives.

I also wrote this letter as a means to nag you from the great beyond. No, you can't escape my nagging, although I prefer to call it "soon-to-be dead wife advice," (you know, this could start a trend).

First of all, get over it, dude, and move on, for heaven's sake. I know you miss me, (you better) but don't be one of those woe-is-me pains in the rear who mopes around the house every day feeling sorry for yourself for the next twenty years. You're way too cool for that.

Jon smiled as he read Anna's letter.

Also, I think you should sell this big old barn. Move somewhere warm, and do some real writing, like all those novels you started and never finished or write those screenplays like you always threatened to do.

Jon sat down on the attic floor and continued to read.

Also, keep exercising, eating right, and watching the Cubs. Find someone you care for (yes, you have my permission) and who cares for you (that's very important). Feel like getting married again? Go for it. If not, live in some sin and have fun. But please, just make sure in either case, she is NOT a f-ing Cardinal fan. You know all those people are innately bad and worship Satan.

Jon laughed out loud and wiped tears from his eyes.

Okay, enough nagging. I never told you this before, but I'd come up here sometimes and read our old love letters from your Nebraska days out loud just to hear your words. They made me smile and cry at the same time. I know, I'm weird. In one of your letters I found this note attached inside. A long time ago, you had asked me to keep it for you, so I did.

Jon took off the paper clip holding a handwritten note.

Based on this note, it looks like you made a promise years ago you may have forgotten. But I know you, if I am not doing well, you won't leave me, no matter what. But if I'm not around, I am asking you, as a favor to me, to please go. Promises need to be kept. Just go, it'll do you good. Take that toy of yours and have a blast. If you don't, you'll regret it and I'll be pissed, and you know what that can be like. Besides, you know I am always right.

Jon nodded, knowing Anna was, in fact, usually right.

Well, you just pulled in the driveway, so I need to go downstairs so you don't think I'm a crazy old lady who sits around all day and reads old love letters. Oh, wait a minute, that is exactly what I am. Anyway, I made spaghetti for tonight and got that good Italian bread and our favorite red wine. No regrets, okay? Love ya, sweetie and have a good trip.

Jon stared at Anna's letter for several minutes. Then read the attached note, which was a reminder of a promise he had made so long ago.

Before he returned the letters to the box that once held them, he discovered a pair of dark blue, woolen gloves. At first, he could not remember where they had come from. Then he did remember ... and smiled.

Later that day, he went to the garage and pulled the tarp off a low-slung car with very cool wheels. He stood back and smiled as if he was seeing an old friend again after ten years. He was a great friend.

The next day, he took the car to his favorite mechanic and said he was going on a cross-country trip and wanted the car checked over from top to bottom. Jon was told to come back in a week and his will would be done.

It was done, and a week later in early June 2016, he backed out of his overly long driveway, which he hated to shovel in the winter, and lowered the convertible top of the now fully serviced muscle car, The GOAT, which seemed as excited to head west as he was.

He looked at the for-sale sign in the front yard and started to remember things. Then he stopped. He had made a promise to Anna and himself that it was time he looked ahead, not back. So, he did the most logical and obvious thing he could do at that moment. He stomped on the accelerator, felt the huge V-8 come to life, and laid two patches of rubber just because it felt so damn good to do so.

JT — As usual, Anna was right. I needed to go. It's not that I really expected anyone to show up, but at least I would have known I kept my promise even if no one else did. Besides, Nebraska was sort of on the way to San Diego, which was kind of, although not really, on the way to Santa Barbara, which I always felt would be a good place to write novels or screenplays. Or both.

I had never forgotten those guys and that time of my life. Yet, the Vietnam War was the reason, either directly or indirectly, all of us ended up together in Nebraska at a college no one had ever heard of.

Hiram Scott had served its purpose and, like scores of other for-profit institutions, closed its doors only a few years after the war ended. Its utility for those who needed a place to go instead of Southeast Asia was no longer required.

To be sure, not all the students chose for-profit colleges as temporary havens from the war, but a large percentage did, and the service those colleges provided, while financially costly, served a definitive if only temporary purpose.

But the incongruity of those colleges was the assumption that they saved the lives of young men who went to a campus rather than a war zone, and as a consequence, lives were saved.

To be sure, *certain* lives were saved, but when draft boards granted a deferment to a young man who could afford to go to a college, any college, a young man who could not afford the tuition was drafted and sent in his place, perhaps to die in a rice paddy. It wasn't fair.

Had I not entered the attic that day and found Anna's reminder of my fifty-year appointment at a bakery in Scottsbluff, I would not have gone back there. But having read my old letters to her, I was reminded of my day-to-day life that year in Nebraska, and my references in those letters to Tony, Augie, Jimmy, Gus, and Alan. In fact, for several nights after reading those letters, I had dreams about those guys, the town, and about the Walker family, who I had lost contact with decades earlier.

After reading the note Anna had saved for me all those years, and what we had all promised to each other that morning in 1966, I was determined to get there.

But it had been so long since that promise was made. So much had happened in the world, and I was sure so much had happened in the lives of all the guys that I knew in my heart only I would show up. But in the end, I didn't really care. All I knew was that I was, in essence, going back in time, and the worst thing that could happen was I might be able to buy some warm donuts on an early morning June day, even if I ate them alone.

Anna had written I'd regret it if I didn't go. She had always said we should live our lives with no regrets; it was a pet phrase of hers, and I knew what she meant. As I tooled along I-80 going eighty miles per hour, the sound of a finely tuned 360 HP tri-power V-8 made me leave the radio off and just listen, as I remembered old friends.

Jon drove the 1967 triple white GTO convertible slowly down Broadway with its top down and a '60s Greatest Hits CD playing. He felt it was the right thing to do. For some fleeting minutes, he felt eighteen again as downtown Scottsbluff appeared through his blue-tinted Ray-Ban Wayfarers.

He kept moving his head from one side of the street to the other and was amazed by the fact many of the old businesses and buildings were still there, just as he remembered them, including a diner, farm feed store, TV repair shop, and most importantly … the bakery. He fought the urge to stop then and there and grab some donuts but resisted the temptation and instead decided to wait until the next morning.

He pulled into an angled parking spot and exited the GOAT into bright afternoon sunlight. He was tan, trim, and wore a blue tennis shirt, golf shorts, and Hoka running shoes.

JT — I've heard our sense of smell is our strongest. I believe it. After all those years, it was a familiar aroma that hit me the hardest, or was it a fragrance? Maybe it was sugar beets or corn or some other elixir indigenous to Western Nebraska, but whatever it was, I remembered and inhaled that smell as I walked down the street.

That day I remembered a quote from Bob Dylan: "Yesterday is just a memory; tomorrow is never what it is supposed to be." I never really got that quote until that day in Scottsbluff. Everything was the same as it had been fifty years ago, except everything was different, including me.

Jon came to the Lincoln Hotel and discovered it had been converted to the Scottsbluff Senior Living Center. After he entered, he looked around and saw two dozen senior citizens sitting quietly talking, reading books, sleeping, or playing cards. A flat-screen TV was on in the corner, showing the game show *Jeopardy*.

JT — When I looked at the same front desk, I saw it clearly from years ago. I envisioned that young girl who checked me in that first day and gave me my room keys. I wondered if I still owed that $5.00 for a lost key. I even remembered her name was Vicki and wondered how in the hell I remembered her name when I seem to forget where I leave my keys, or wallet, and everything else on a daily basis now.

As I gawked around the lobby, I was approached by the young lady who had been behind the desk. "Sir, can I help you find someone?"

"Oh, I'm sorry, I was just remembering. I used to live here when this was a college dorm about a hundred years ago."

"Actually, it was more like fifty years ago. By the way, my name is Elaine Webb. I'm the assistant manager of this facility."

"Hi, my name is Jon Taylor. I'm just visiting and stopped in to experience some déjà vu. You're right about the fifty years, but the place looks about the same, except for the age of the residents."

"Welcome back. I'm so glad you stopped in. Yes, this place was constructed very well. I think it will last another hundred years."

"When I was here this lobby was always packed, and I recall there was a jukebox over in the corner there. I was up in Room 338 and stole the key as a memento when I left in 1966."

"You know, Room 338 is vacant if you would like to go up and see it while you're here."

"Really? That would be terrific, if it's no trouble."

"No trouble at all. Let me go get the key for you."

JT — When I got on the elevator, there was that smell thing again. That damn elevator smelled exactly the same as it did the first time I got on in 1965. Or did I just want to believe that? No, it definitely smelled the same. I think.

As I walked toward Room 338, I remembered that first day hauling my two suitcases and duffle bag down that hallway. I was sincerely hoping that any minute in 2016, I was going to see Tony fly out the door. He didn't.

The room was furnished with a couch, love seat, dining room set, flat-screen TV, and assorted odds and ends. It looked far neater and cleaner than it was when Tony, Augie, and I lived there.

After shutting the door, I roamed around the rooms, and everything seemed smaller than I remembered. One thing that stuck out was that in what was once my bedroom, there was an old desk there, and I was sure it was the one I had used to write to Anna … once a week.

Before I finally left the room, I turned back and replayed scenes of Tony and Augie beating the crap out of each other half a century before. I suddenly hoped that at least one of them would show up the next morning.

"Thanks for taking the time to let me see that room. That was very kind of you. It's been fifty years and sometimes you need to actually see things from your past to prove to yourself they were real."

"No problem at all. Very glad you came to visit, and I hope you enjoy your stay in town."

"Thank you."

Jon started to leave but stopped with one more question. "Elaine, have you ever heard of a guy around here named Alan Jordan?"

"As in Jordan Enterprises?"

"I would guess that's Alan. Does he still live around here?"

"He owns a big ranch outside town. I heard it's a few thousand acres, but we don't see him in town much anymore."

"What does Jordan Enterprises do?"

"A bit of everything from what I can tell. All I know is he owns a private jet, a G something …"

"A G-5?"

"Yes, I think that is it. He flies all over the world but comes back here every fall to watch football over in Lincoln. He's a big Cornhusker fan. He'll spend a month or so here until the weather turns cold, and he'll take off to somewhere that's warm."

"Thanks again for the info. I've taken enough of your time."

"Stop in anytime, and welcome back."

When Jon left, Elaine stared out the window and watched Jon disappear down the street.

> JT — After leaving Elaine, I walked down Broadway and eventually under the marquee of the Midwest Theater. I tried to remember how many times in that one year we had watched a film in that place but couldn't. All I could recall was it was a lot, and that place had great popcorn.
>
> A few minutes later, I entered the park where the guys had set up their Red Cross tent in a sincere effort to prevent breast cancer and protect women's health. Even back then, their effort did not work with the school, which expelled them, or the police, who arrested them, and a local judge gave them each a month in jail.
>
> Still, their creativity and money-making plan earned them undying respect from the guys in school, except a guy from Ohio who found out his sister had been "examined" by one of the guys and they charged her $10 for the privilege. He was pissed, but even he had to admit it was a pretty good business model.
>
> After walking around the park, I finally found what I was looking for. It was the ten-foot tree that Jimmy had stuffed a white bag with two glazed donuts into. That tree was now thirty feet tall, but the hole was still visible, only twenty feet higher. I assumed the donuts were a bit stale after fifty years.

Jon sat on the park bench for nearly two hours after finding the tree and remembered lots of "stuff." Finally, as the sun was beginning to sink, he got up and walked back to the GTO.

> JT — Talking to Elaine at the senior citizen center, and hearing about Alan, made me regret that I hadn't done my homework on the net

before coming to Scottsbluff. Maybe even reaching out to the guys and trying to convince them to keep their fifty-year-old promises or even to determine if any of them were still alive.

But then reality set in, and I realized even if the guys were alive, the idea of anyone showing up the next morning was a romantic pipe dream fueled by the letters I had read, Anna's encouragement to keep a promise, and a writer's creative brain. I wanted it to be but knew in my heart it would not be.

I finally decided that I was going to leave that afternoon and head west to San Diego rather than waste a night in Scottsbluff. But then I walked back under the marquee of the Midwest Theater and saw they were running a "classic" film that night. *The Good, the Bad, and the Ugly.* Obviously, I couldn't miss that. But I promised myself I was not going to get up at sunrise the next morning and go to a damn bakery and wait for a bunch of guys from fifty years ago who would never show up anyway. That would be weird.

The next morning before sunrise, Jon checked out of his Holiday Inn Express and walked nearly a half a mile to his destination. Broadway was deserted except for delivery trucks making their early morning rounds.

JT — After buying my dozen donuts, still warm, I tried to find the exact same spot where the five of us had been sitting fifty years ago, to the minute. While searching for that exact spot, I saw the red brick that was still holding the door open, so I knew I had found the right spot. No question.

Jon sat on the curb, his legs stretched out, and thought back to 1966.

JT — As I ate my first donut, I looked across the street and could envision Augie, Tony, Jimmy, Gus, and Alan walking down the street as the brothers pounded the hell out of each other. It was then I wished I had tried to contact them.

After the sun rose and it was clear no one was showing up, I did not regret that I had stayed over the night. First of all, the movie and popcorn were great, but had I left the night before, I would have always wondered if, in fact, I had been the only one *not* to show up.

I concluded the fantasy that I had conjured up in my writer's brain regarding some kind of mini reunion needed a definitive ending. The reality and clarity that morning often brings led me to realize that the one year at Hiram Scott in Western Nebraska had made a greater impression on me than the other guys.

But I was okay with that. I would have liked to have seen them just to know they were okay, and their lives were full, and they were happy, but I guess I could always assume that was the case for all the guys, which was almost as good.

In the end, maybe not knowing all the potential bad things that could have befallen my friends over fifty years was better than knowing.

Sometimes memories are best left alone. To revisit them can be risky, even painful. But in the case of a fifty-year-old memory of eating a warm glazed donut sitting on a Scottsbluff curb on a spring morning, I had to admit the warm glazed donut tasted as good as the memory.

When Jon reached in the white bag for a second donut, he heard a voice behind him. "You gonna eat all those things yourself, or you gonna share?"

Without turning around, Jon lifted the bag over his head in offering to the voice.

"Thanks, been in town long?" the voice asked.

"Without sounding too poetic, in a way, I never left."

"That does sound a bit poetic. Can tell you're a writer. I always knew you would be."

"To be more precise I became a journalist, never the novelist or screenwriter I wanted to be."

"It's not too late. You're good. I read your stuff online all the time."

"Someone else used to tell me that."

"Sorry about Anna. I seem to remember you writing to her all the time."

"Not as much as she wrote me."

"She must have liked something you wrote; she stayed with you for forty-five years."

"How do you know that?"

"I know stuff."

Alan sat down next to Jon at the curb. Both men stared straight across the street where the old Western Auto had been.

"I was across the street in a doorway. Wasn't sure how long you had been here. Wanted to give you a chance to think a little bit on your own."

"Think anyone else will show?"

"They won't."

"You mean …?"

"Yeah."

> JT — Alan and I walked slowly down Broadway past the Midwest Theater and ended up at the city park, where we sat on a bench as the sun rose. We recalled how each of us had talked about our plans for the future that morning exactly fifty years before.

No shit, I'm going to be a fucking hero. I mean it. I'm going to kill me a bunch of commies, get medals and …

> JT — In late June of 1966, less than a month after leaving Scottsbluff and returning to the great state of New Jersey for the summer, and only three weeks before he was supposed to report to the marines, Tony was hit by a car that had run up on the curb in front of an Italian restaurant in Trenton. He was pinned under the car for over an hour as paramedics tried to remove him. In the process, he suffered severe burns on his back from the tailpipe of the car, and his screams of pain lasted until he finally passed out. Later at the hospital, his left leg was amputated just above the knee. As a result, he never killed any commies, never got his judo studio, nor became a Hollywood star. Instead, he became a bouncer in a strip club and a part-time bookmaker.

After I graduate from college, I've decided to join the Peace Corps. I heard it's hard … besides, I could never really shoot anyone.

> JT — After Augie graduated from Penn State University in 1971, earning a degree in Social Studies, he was drafted before he could join the Peace Corps. He thought of going to Canada but instead entered

Officer Candidate School and went into the army as a first lieutenant. He rose to the rank of major after entering the Green Berets.

During his three tours of duty, he earned two Purple Hearts, a Silver Star, and The Congressional Medal of Honor for his heroic actions, including saving four of his fellow soldiers during a firefight in Cambodia. He appeared on over a dozen talk shows, several magazine covers, and three films … playing a soldier.

A week after Augie received his Medal of Honor, at an event attended by his brother, Tony shot himself in the head and died in Augie's arms. He had never gotten over the fact that Augie had lived his dream. Augie died five years later from complications from inhaling Agent Orange while in Vietnam. Neither man ever married and instead "gave all the women a chance."

All I want is my shot in the NBA and show the world what I can do. People don't care what color you are in the NBA.

JT — Jimmy entered the NBA in 1967 after being drafted by the 76ers and became an immediate star. His on-court talent, outgoing personality, humor, and charisma made him famous all over the country.

In 1971, the Philadelphia 76ers played the Boston Celtics in Boston Gardens, and Jimmy stole the show. He scored twenty-eight points, including the game winner, had eleven rebounds, and twelve assists. The Triple Double.

After that game with the Celtics, Jimmy was walking to the team bus when he was shot in the back of the head, murdered by a Boston woman who later claimed Jimmy had killed her son. She said Jimmy had drowned him.

When Mom passes, I want to go to Harvard or Yale and get my MBA. Go to work on Wall Street and make a million bucks before I'm thirty.

JT — Alan never made it to Harvard or Yale but traveled the globe and made a lot more than a million dollars. He did so by selling Center Pivot Irrigation systems to third world countries all over the planet. Eventually he bought the company and, after six years, took it public. He acquired over a dozen other agricultural-related firms from around the world and sold that international conglomerate to another international conglomerate and banked over a billion dollars. In cash. Alan never married, although he had many deep and meaningful relationships with women over seven continents. They were particularly deep.

After having their two-donut allotment, Alan and Jon walked through the city park and talked.

JT — It had been fifty years, but Alan and I fell back into a familiar pattern of conversation like it had been a single day. We walked around town and saw buildings that unlike us had not changed at all.

Alan had stayed in shape but had filled out in the shoulders, and his now graying hair gave him a sophisticated look. He had thrown away his glasses for contact lenses and had gotten dental implants that befitted his corporate image. Especially when it came to being on the cover of *Fortune* magazine.

But he maintained after all those years that almost imperceptible swagger when he walked, like that of a professional athlete. Nothing obnoxious, just the walk of a guy who was sure of himself. The exact kind of walk he had when I met him in 1965.

"After I heard of Jimmy's death, I checked out Augie and Tony and learned they died years ago too. You were easier to keep track of, given your columns," Alan said as the men walked past the old Armory, which still sported three American flags on rusty poles.

"Anna and I were in Italy for a month when Jimmy was killed. We purposely kind of tuned out the news, and I did not hear about it at first, and when I did, I only heard of a basketball player who had been shot and killed. I didn't think of it being Jimmy, our Jimmy. As far as Augie and Tony were concerned, I had no idea how to reach them."

"I know a lot of guys I met at Hiram Scott came out here to stay out of the draft. But it was only a temporary reprieve. I learned over a hundred guys were eventually drafted from 1966 to 1975, and twenty-one of them from around here got killed. A bunch of other guys were messed up emotionally and mentally after they came home," Alan said.

"I got drafted in 1974 after grad school, but the war was winding down by then. I got a desk job writing PR releases in Washington, DC," Jon said.

After making their way around town, Alan and Jon returned to the park and sat down on a green park bench and watched some ducks swim and kids play in the lily-covered pond.

"My mom's illness hung on for ten more years as medicines got better, but she never made it out of a wheelchair. I was her only caregiver, so I got a draft deferment."

"So, why the hell did you come back today?" Jon asked.

"I was hoping you would be here."

"Why didn't you contact me as we got closer to the date?"

"I wanted to see," Alan said.

"See what?"

"See if that time back then meant the same to you as it did to me."

"I have a feeling Tony, Augie, and Jimmy would have been here if they could have."

"Gus too," Alan added.

"Just think, if we hadn't gone to the lake that day, Gus and Jimmy might still be around."

"I'm not so sure," Alan said.

"What do you mean?"

"Seems no matter what you do or where you go, fate has a plan for you. You can try to pull a fake on fate, like going to Nebraska, or Boston, or Europe, but fate, as someone once said, is a bitch. Seems like she'll track you down and make sure you get what you're supposed to get."

"Getting kind of philosophical in your old age, aren't you?"

"What about you? I read that thing you wrote a few weeks ago about making plans. Maybe at our ages we all get philosophical," Alan noted.

"Yeah, maybe."

As if of one mind, the men rose off the park bench and began a slow stroll back to Broadway Street while a warm sun heated the cool air and foretold of a bright afternoon. "By the way, did you and Anna have any kids?"

"No, we tried like hell, but no," Jon said.

"So, what the hell do you want to do when you grow up?"

"I was going to tackle the Great American novel for about the fifth time, but I took some script writing classes at Northwestern's Film School and think I'm going to write scripts instead."

"What do you do after you write scripts?"

"Try to sell the damn thing to a studio."

Alan suddenly stopped on the sidewalk and turned to Jon. "Any money in that?"

"Sure, for the studio."

"What's it cost to make a movie?"

"Depends."

"On what?"

"The script, the budget, the cast, location, director. Lots of variables."

"You should write a script about Hiram Scott. About the guys we knew, the war, all the stuff that happened back then," Alan suggested.

"Not a bad idea," Jon said.

"I know the war had a lot to do with some guys coming here, but it seems each guy had his own different reasons," Alan mused.

"Tell you what, I'll write the script if you help me remember some of the stuff; then you and I can go to LA and meet with the studios and see if we can raise the money."

"I thought you said the studios make all the money."

"They do."

"What would it cost to make your script into a movie, you know, make the movie ourselves?"

"I don't know, maybe ten to twelve million, depending on above the line."

"What's above the line mean?"

"It's mainly the actors, writers, directors, and producers."

For several moments it appeared Alan was calculating numbers in his head while early morning shoppers and donut buyers walked around the two men who were facing each other and deep in conversation.

"You mean, we could make a real movie, one that would play in theaters for only twelve million dollars?"

"Sure," Jon said.

"Could I be in it?"

"I guess, but I'd have to write a part for a Danny DeVito type."

"Fuck you. I do have other attributes, you know."

"Oh yeah, I remember you standing on that chair."

"Ah yes, one of my finest moments. Okay, here's the deal. You write scripts, and I'll put up the cash, and we'll split everything fifty-fifty."

"You're nuts. It's not that easy."

"Why not?"

"We'd need to hire a producer, figure out distribution, get a casting agent, a good attorney—there are lots of moving parts."

Again, moving as one, the men continued their walk down Broadway. Alan stared down at the pavement deep in thought while Jon continued to take in the sights of Scottsbluff he had forgotten but now looked familiar.

"Look, I took a small company with a negative net worth and in twelve years sold it for over 1.2 billion. Also negotiated for myself a ten-year, seven-figure consulting contract with the company I sold it to and acquired a dozen other firms over the years that all make substantial annual profits. Whatever we need to do, we will do. Whoever we need to hire, we will hire."

This time it was Jon who stopped and turned to Alan. "Are you fucking serious about all this?"

"Fifty years ago, you and I worked together to get a few dozen of our classmates through college. I don't see any difference now, just more zeros."

"Yeah, a lot more zeros. What if the scripts are crap, the movies suck, and we lose money?"

"You don't have any idea how much money I make a year, do you? No, of course you don't. But making a dozen films that all lose money over the next few years could offset the capital gains I make every year. In short, I won't miss the cash; in fact, my accountants, of which there are ten, would like to see the losses. Any other questions?"

"Okay, but I want to make good movies and make money," Jon said.

"Damn, you can't take yes for an answer, can you?"

"I just want you to understand the risks."

"That's another reason I want to partner with you. You do care about the risks. Plus, I love how you write, always have. Always thought you were wasting your time at a newspaper."

Jon and Alan continued their stroll down Broadway in silence for several minutes. Finally, Jon had another question. "Where do you live?"

"Everywhere."

"To write a script about Hiram Scott, I'd want to stay around town for a few weeks to talk to some people who were here fifty years ago. Get some background info."

"I have a great guesthouse at my little place just outside town. Even has a pool. But in the winter, we can go down to my place in Key West. Have my own landing strip there. You can channel Hemingway there while you sit on my lanai, look at the ocean, and dream up stories we can make movies out of."

"You know this is fucking nuts, right?"

"I waited fifty years to see if you'd show up at a donut shop at six in the morning and you did. Appears to me, I was a pretty good judge of character back then. Look, fuck the money, let's go have some fun in the time we have left and make some damn movies."

The men continued their walk down Broadway and stopped under the Midwest Theater marquee.

"You know, we could have our premiers right here," Jon said.

"Damn good idea, but I would've thought of that myself, you know."

"Sure, you would've. Who do you want playing you in our first film about our time at dear old Hiram Scott College?"

"Brad Pitt," Alan seriously said.

"You're kidding me."

"No, I'm not kidding. I think I look a lot like him."

"I can tell I should be in charge of casting all our movies."

"We'll make it a team effort," Alan suggested.

"Too bad Tony isn't around. He could be our first star."

"'Fuck yeah, Jersey boy,'" Alan said, sounding not at all like Tony.

As the men continued their walk, a black 1949 Cadillac convertible with a red leather interior and the rumble of two four-barrel carbs pulled up to the curb. The driver was an attractive woman in her late fifties whose blonde hair was pulled back in a bun. She wore Ray-Bans and a silk scarf around her neck.

"Hey, Doc, how's it going?" Alan said.

"Hi, Alan, things are fine. Who is your friend there? He looks a little familiar."

"Yeah, I think you might know him. But I bet he doesn't recognize you."

Jon's face went from curious to stunned as he stood on the sidewalk taking in the banter between Alan and the driver of the classic Caddy with cool wheels.

Alan continued talking while Jon struggled to get his mouth moving. "I think you two single folks should chat for a while. Maybe you have some stuff to talk about while driving in that fancy car. I'm going to go back to my office and investigate buying a little film studio somewhere. I'll meet you guys back at La Bonita for lunch at one. I'm buying, 'cause I'm really rich."

"Sounds like a plan, Alan." Turning to his tongue-tied companion, she added, "Hi, Jon, you going to climb in, or are you afraid of women drivers?"

"Nan, is that you?"

"Officially, it's Dr. Nancy Walker Connor, pediatric neurosurgeon. But Nan still works for old friends. Alan, you were right. I think he is surprised."

Alan smiled at two old friends reuniting and decided they needed some time alone to catch up on fifty years. As he walked away, he pulled out his cell phone and took the first steps toward acquiring a small film production company in Burbank.

A stunned Jon climbed into the Cadillac. "How did you know I was …?"

"You met my daughter Elaine yesterday. Her residency included working in senior facilities."

"Daughter?"

"Yes, she recognized your name since my family talked a lot about you over the years. My parents thought the world of you. We also had a picture of you that my brother, Ethan, took that Christmas day."

"Ethan?"

"Yes, he's an attorney in Denver and … Look, just sit back, relax, and let's drive out to the bluffs and catch up before lunch. By the way, I'm glad you're back in town, because you owe me a turkey dinner."

Jon sat back and smiled as the Cadillac drove past the bakery and the Beach Boys' "Wouldn't It Be Nice" played on the radio.

ACKNOWLEDGMENT

Writing fiction, even historical fiction, is the ultimate time machine. It can take us backward or forward in time. It can allow us to revisit old friends and events or deliver us to yet unmet people or situations. It can scare us, make us laugh, cry, make us regret or anticipate. All we must do as writers is to sit down and write, and we can go anywhere, with anyone, and create the world we want.

That is the fun part. Looking forward to going to bed early so you can wake up early and write is a gift. You don't have to be a Shakespeare or Byron or Tennessee Williams or Capote or King to enjoy the process. But when you put the pen down (or in today's world close your computer), someone must take what you have created, be it good or bad, and do something with it.

For me, whether it is writing a script or a novel, that person is Linda Jordan. Linda and I have been working together for ten years, although we had met years before that when she was a legal assistant in the law firm I used. Since then, she has become a close friend to my son, Matt, my wife, Marsha, and me, plus the person I turn to and leave in possession of my writing.

In the time since, Linda has become a partner, and I have learned every writer, be they famous or anonymous, has a "Linda" they can turn to. A Linda they can trust. So, while many people of various skill sets are required to create any book, I wanted to acknowledge that in my case Linda is my go-to, and for that I am grateful.

Thanks, Lin … you're the best.

About The Author

For Mark Donahue, thirty years in senior management at two Fortune 200 firms was enough. So, he quit and decided at long last to *write*. The result has been five best-selling novels released in 2020; several more awaiting publication; and seventeen screenplays, one of which is in pre-production as a feature film. "Guess I should have left commercial real estate sooner." His readers wholeheartedly agree.

Mark resides in Southwestern Ohio with wife, Marsha; Mika, The Wonder Dog; Whirling Dervish Gracie; and New-Kid-on-the-Block, Max. The former "Boss of the House," Rocky the Cat, sleeps comfortably in the shade of his favorite tree; and the late, great Carly (of *Last at Bat* fame) watches over all of them from her honored perch on a bookshelf—where else would a writer's dog be?

www.DonahueLiteraryProperties.com

www.MarkRDonahue.com